Handel

OPULICHE

PK DAVIDS

HANDELBOOK
www.hbooknetworks.com

PK Davids

Opuliche

A Handel book

HANDEL African Library of Fiction
Pauline Kanene Davids
Opuliche
Copyright © Pauline Kanene Davids

2008 International Edition
Published by
The African Books Network
Handel Books Limited
6/9 Handel Avenue
AI EBS Nigeria WA
Email: handelbook@yahoo.co.uk

Marketing and Distribution in the U.S. UK,
Europe, N. America (US and Canada),
and Commonwealth countries outside Africa by
African Books Collective Ltd.
PO Box 721
Oxford OX1 9EN
UK
Email: orders@africanbookscollective.com

ISBN: 978-9-7835-0622-0

A Handel Books Publication

Opuliche is the story of every woman who must struggle through an old tradition of boy child preference. From conception, and its attendant worries for a male child, through birth and training, the African woman has squarely faced what seems a man's world with its benign disregard for the girl child. Here is one who struggles to overcome... Her courage and triumph in the face of all odds should be the hope of all women of character this side of the world.

INTRODUCTION
A STORY OF COURAGE AND TRIUMPH

*A*lthough *Opuliche* was published only in the year 2002, its completion had taken place back in 1976 as the Davids manuscripts attest. Two whole decades and half had elapsed before its first publication and yet, as fiction, it was still necessary to protect the privacy of some people and communities as evident in the imaginary towns and villages in the novel: Ogu, Ndudi, Okpu, Nsu, etc. These contrast with actual places: Enugu, Nnobi and Aba south east Nigeria. There is also a mix of real and contrived names such as Angelina, Modiba, Dobendu, Mama Antoni, Venni, etc. The use of real and fictional names in the novel is thus significant as it allays the danger of discrepancy which can easily arise from the many cases of authorial opinions, judgments and cross narratives which abound in the story.

Then it is evident from the Davids narrative that Opuliche was a real person, if not the author of the story herself, raised in the gloomy times of colonial rule where missionary activities grappled with traditional ways of life. Ogu, the fictional birthplace of Opuliche, was understandably a society on the throes of change even as the people appeared steeped in traditional ways. Thus when Modiba is reported to have fallen back, dejected at her birth of the baby Opuliche, after the good neighbour, Ohuka, had replied to her question with the brusque exclamation: "It's a girl," we must not see the action as a future sign of poor parenting or the spite of a wicked neighbour. On the contrary we are ready for the contrast of traditional opinion and behaviours with the positive capabilities of the girl hero who has just come.

Davids divides her novel in two parts, each containing short episodic chapters and incidents that inspire compulsive reading. Part One, containing a prologue and eleven chapters, shows Opuliche's birth and her early upbringing by her parents, Modiba and Dobendu. Although both parents had wanted a male child, Opuliche is fervently loved and cared for. As usual in traditional societies, the maternal presence looms large; it is the guide and strict disciplinary influence on youngsters, male and female. Through Modiba, the young Opuliche is to adopt the resilient and determined attitude that will see her through her many struggles. And with her sudden exit from the world, our pathetic Opuliche is to learn the ropes through some hard personal decisions that she had imbibed from her mother.

Part Two, also comprising eleven chapters, further chronicles Opuliche's travails through school. In fact the entire Opuliche story seems to be the ordeals and struggles of a young woman to acquire education. Modiba's early death in the first section is closely followed by Dobendu's transition in the second part of the story. This is rendered by the author in a manner that heightens the tragic dimension of Opuliche's life. With the death of her father Opuliche's travails are further worsened by penury and frustrations with college authorities.

Opuliche's school adventures, which her story truly encapsulates, are told by Davids with quaint, illustrative details that evoke memories of austere, provincial lifestyles.

> The town of Ogu was made up of several villages including
> Ogu and Ndudi. Ndudi on the opposite side was a forest village
> shielded with large baobab trees....The general belief in Ndudi
> was that the next-door neighbour must be out to undo one's
> own family. So the watchword was always 'beware never
> befriend.' (22)

Here tradition is evidently the hard but disciplined way and
must either blend in tenuous demands of missionary education
and modern livelihood or give way entirely. The author is
hardly on the side of any of both modern or traditional life
ways. Rather she is a commentator on a history of personal
struggles. What conclusions we derive from her many censures
– as in the criticism of convent traditions, the complex of 'holy
Nweje' or Opuliche's killing of the sacred snake – can only be
obvious from our own intense reading and response to the
story. Yet Davids is particularly successful in the exposition of
traditional and colonial flaws in a way that often reveals her
strong capacity for liberated thinking:

> The few girls who had been in the convent for some years often
> threatened the new boys' school girls with severe punishment from
> the sisters because of their rawness and lack of manners. 'You're very
> rude,' they would complain.
> 'You have no manners Opuliche,' the reformed, tame and polished
> girls would reprimand her. 'Can't you say please?'
> Opuliche will hear this scolding ten times in an hour. She would
> watch the tame girls twist their mouths in distaste. (57)

While her omniscient narrative style allows for authorial

interjections and explanations that characterise most biographical narratives, the story teller also shows some craft in handling these comments to the overall didactic purpose of her story:

> This convent type of celibacy was brought from outside Africa. It was a strange notion that bred many desperate and unhappy women. At the end those relatives that she had trained usually despised the 'holy nweje' girl. They would even make fun of her single status. They would shun her in her old age. At this point, the holy nweje girl could be any thing but happy. Children were so important in the life of the average woman that a woman could be mother of her children without being married. However, Holy Nweje wouldn't know until they got to the dead end. What a fix for the proud, good and holy nweje girl! (95)

Today's school girls and boys will be fascinated to read Opuliche's struggle to acquire education in those years. Her embarrassing fall while returning from a local stream at Adazi, with her bucket trailing her descent down the hill, reminds us of series of similar events in real life accounts. When she ate a whole pot of rice all alone in the night, only to demand from Celibret a few hours later who did this to her, she was acting out a familiar chapter in our own youths when we found consolation in our favourite meals. For some of us, it was eba and vegetable soup and we could never stop eating this delicacy. One colleague in my school days, who must not be named here, had written a whole poem which stated that when he saw a cow eating grass he would immediately think of *Afang* soup!

There are several more serious chapters on Opuliche's

growth and development. The burial of her father in her absence and her lone fight against this practice that disregards the female member of the household are two cases that draw our sympathy firmly on the side of the heroine. No doubt there is always the compulsion of reading Feminist theories in novels by African women writers, especially where traditional practices are sorely criticised, but there are other important insights to the Opuliche story. For example, the comments on some missionary sisters in this book is an indictment of their religion and its proselytising mission in Africa. This may seem to justify later Nigerian government decision to take over the running of missionary schools at the time. Incidents of the prejudice and bigotry of some reverend sisters or the strange morality of 'holy Nweje' girls form important sub themes of the novel. These are aspects of colonial mentality inhered in African nation states. Reading Opuliche's and her friends' experiences, one is tempted to wonder if the blind zealotry fed by religious education should always be swallowed with no second thoughts. In other words, how much of our 'common sense' – which by the way is not common, as a famed teacher would say – must we suspend in the name of religious or any followership? This, too, is another significant sidebar to the Davids story.

We have to follow our child hero, Opuliche, as she traverses the stage of innocence only to be launched unceremoniously into adulthood and its travails. We join to laugh at her follies and tend to cry with her as she grapples with her many frustrations and disappointments. All these are told in rapid and mingled succession of events and thoughts. It is remarkable that Opuliche has such a quick narrative pace; thus a whole life account is rendered in just over one hundred pages. Where other writers would fill tons of epic details, Davids cuts through unnecessary hagiographic tedium and compresses her narration. The result is a compact life account of twenty-two short chapters whose prologue deigns to introduce a story of female child discrimination while the entire story achieves the opposite effect of female triumph and achievement.

The epilogue bears witness to a most revolutionary redefinition of self from one of acquiescence to tradition and custom to the firm belief in one's intuition and sense of familial identity. In rejecting discriminatory practices by religious denominations and also the traditional endorsement of those often mistaken oracular proclamations on our destiny, Davids shows us that we men or women, like Opuliche, are really the ones in control of our beliefs and, thenceforth, destiny:

> From that day, Opuliche started to think that this woman, who used to get the 'truth' from the oracle, must have not been a good friend of Mohiba. 'Otherwise, why should the oracle say that the son was my father while this next one was not my mother? Perhaps the problem was with the oracle,' she summed it all up.
>
> So in baptising the child, Opuliche called her Modiba. The name Modiba, added to the child's first name, was to honour Opuliche's mother. To her, the little baby girl was Modiba and no other. The woman she had known and loved for but some brief time in her life had every reason to return to her. (137)

With her children named after the two most important people in her life: father and mother, Opuliche leaves us with the proverbial wisdom of the triumph of all good things over challenges of fate and circumstance. Thus whether explicit or subtly contrived in the actions of Davids' girl character, the discerning reader is sure to glean a few gems of wisdom from the adventures of Opuliche. These are no doubt cut from the larger cloak of experience with which this remarkable writer invokes the theme of female educational empowerment with self assurance.

Opuliche, Pauline Davids' female creation, may well represent the classic heroine of modern African writing. It is the story of every woman who must struggle through an old tradition of boy child preference. From conception and its attendant worries for a male child, through birth and training, the African woman has squarely faced what seems a man's world with its benign disregard for the girl child. Here is one who struggles to overcome the obvious disadvantages of being born and raised in a patriarchal male-conditioned society. Her courage and triumph in the face of all odds should be the hope of all women of character this side of the world.

Chin Ce

Dedication

In affectionate memory of my father
Okpala Davids.

A Female!

It was a very dark night. So Modiba had to light her own-made candle light. She could not afford the bush lamp or a cigarette tin lantern. Both of them use kerosene. She had some palm leaves that had been soaked in oil and left in a broken clay pot for several days. This was her candle.

Okori Nwichi, the local seer and gynaecologist, had said that Modiba shall be delivered of two babies: a boy and a girl. Since the sun went down, the labour pains had been heavy. It was literally cooking all parts of her body. She was restless. Feeling like relieving herself in the toilet, she very quickly padded to the nearby bush.

'Don't go too far in the bush, I beg you-o!' Ohuka, her neighbour experienced in child delivery, shouted in alarm. It would be unheard-of for Modiba to deliver her two babies in the bush instead of the usual back yard of the house.

More lighted sticks were brought to add to the ones that came from Modiba's hut as she returned from the bush. Still there was no sign of the twin babies. Ndubisi, the old husband of Ohuka knew much about child delivery too. He was called in at once. Carrying his own candle, he quickly tottered to the scene. Modiba had seen the first signs of labour, but the pains she was experiencing were 'at the wrong place,' she exclaimed in agitation. Instead of the back, the pains came right in front, Modiba complained.

'Maybe this is how twins show their own labour signs before coming out,' said Ohuka. 'It must be the other male.'

Everyone nodded hopefully, especially since a male child was seriously expected. Male children in the land brought complete satisfaction for a married couple. It was the ultimate joy to get a male child. In fact, to deliver a female child gave nobody joy. 'The labour's made easy,' the unhappy husband would say in consolation. He will quickly take comfort in the fact that the life of the mother was preserved in the whole misadventure. 'Perhaps her next baby would be a boy,' he would murmur hopefully to himself. One might have to ask two to three times, before the father would carelessly answer, 'Oh she's got a female.' However, if the baby was a male child, the father would not just say to people: 'my wife has delivered,' he would announce proudly: 'My wife has delivered a son; oh yes a male child!'

It was the tradition of the people to regard a female child without real interest for after all, they reasoned, a woman was meant for another man's compound. That referred to the custom of selling women and making money in the name of bride price. After the bride price was paid, the woman became a complete stranger in her father's home, because she now belonged to her new husband and his family. As a wife, her new family expected a lot from the marriage, part of which was filling the homestead with male children.

This was the cause of Modiba's anxiety. She was apprehensive that her baby may not turn out a male child after all. But Okiri Nwichi had assured her that she would have a set of twins – boy and girl! But what if they were girls, she reasoned in horror. What if Okiri Nwichi had made a mistake? Had his predictions ever been false?

'Are you sleeping or what?' Ohuka's voice snapped at her. Modiba felt a sharp sting on her laps just as Ndubisi gave her a slap to wake her up.

'Your baby is coming now,' Ndubisi announced shortly. 'Put your attention here and do as you're told. Woman, where is the hot water?' he shouted at Ohuka who had gone inside the room to fetch the steaming charcoal pot of hot water.

Modiba was in excruciating pain, but her anxiety over the sex of the coming babies made the pain insignificant. After some time, she heard the yell of a newborn. Her pains were over. She fell back unto the makeshift bed on the floor in exhaustion. Then suddenly rousing herself: 'What is it?' she questioned meaning: did she deliver a male or female? She did not bother to ask if it was twins; she was sure she had delivered only one baby.

There was no answer to her question. The women and Ndubisi were busy cleaning the baby up. Some were getting ready the banana leaves on which the baby and mother would rest for the next eight days *Omugwo*. She requested for some water, and after drinking, Modiba repeated the question: 'What's the sex of the child?'

'It is a female!' came the curt reply from Ohuka.

'Oh,' Modiba exclaimed in a low, dejected voice and fell back to the floor with tears in her eyes.

 **Part One**

1

Growing Up

It used to amuse Modiba how the old ones especially Mama Ohuka would now call her child Ogonnaya, the in-law of her father, when it seemed only yesterday that they had welcomed the child with hardly disguised disdain. Opuliche, as the baby was later named by Dobendu, her father, was growing robust and beautiful by the day. Consultation with the local seer had been made soon after the delivery and it was said that Opuliche was the incarnation of Modiba's late brother. Modiba hailed from Okpu a village which lay several kilometres from Modiba's husband's Ndudi village in Ogu town. These people were such great farmers that they never lacked what to eat but could feed their neighbours. Besides they were also more hospitable than their neighbours.

The town of Ogu was made up of several villages including Ogu and Ndudi. Ndudi on the opposite side was a forest village shielded with large baobab trees. Surrounded by a swamp, fat millipedes made their rounds all over the villages and frightened both children and adults even on their sleeping mats. Poverty and disease were constant guests on the doorposts of the people resulting in their apparent malnourished looks. They seemed to hold a stern distrust for each other.

The general belief in Ndudi was that the next-door neighbour must be out to undo one's own family. So the watchword was always 'beware never befriend.' If one looked relaxed or wore a calm face, that one was dismissed for a fool. A familiar saying was: 'Only fools look with their eyes; wise men always look through the corner of their eyes.' One who appeared always pensive and never glad was regarded as the intelligent person. Someone once remarked that grumbling was the approved and proper use of the two opposite blades across the part of the face called the mouth. The type of names known to people of that time and place were names showing regret, uncertainty, doubt and negative consolation like Olebunne (All in doubt), Nkemechina (That mine is not lost), Ndidi (To endure all). But who could blame the people of Ndudi that much of ignorance and superstition was their lot in this village.

The positive reputation of Opuliche's mother's village seemed to be the only factor that allowed her husband's kindred to give her some benefit of doubt. Otherwise for having a girl child in the first pregnancy she was already doomed to live out her life in condemnation. The signs of hostility had begun immediately after Opuliche's birth but whittled as Modiba grew rich in farming work and generosity. Modiba's depressed spirit was enlivened by the revelation that she was the support of the household. It was a thing of pride that Okpu were people of great and unmatched devotion to work. Mohiba would smile each time she recalled how her husband's people would call her Nwa Okpu akputakpu: people with strong resolve and determination. Moreover, her late brother, was he not the strongest and most enterprising youth, before death cut him down? Her brother had been very dear to her while he lived. And they so loved and supported each other. Modiba quickly transferred this affection to her Opuliche. As far as she was concerned, her daughter held a promise of greater things.

Opuliche did not know the parents of her mother, both being dead before she was born. But she knew Ojaa, her mother's uncle. She also knew Agha, her mother's sister. Modiba used to keep Opuliche in Agha's hut whenever she went to Oku for a visit. Aholum was also a member of the family. Opuliche identified him with the life of her immediate family. As far as she could remember, he had always been there. Her mother used to call him *Nnaa*. Modiba believed that Aholum was the spirit of her dead father which came back to life.

Opuliche feared her mother Mohiba but loved her father Dobendu, the great tailor of Ndudi village in Ogu. Although of average height, his slim build lent him more height than his equals. He had attended the mission school as a youth and was able to speak a little English. The villagers respected him for this ability which was a rare feat in those days. As a tailor he did not live in his village but a nearby town called Ahianwama. He was said to be living 'abroad.' He had many apprentices. These boys, some who had come from faraway Uga, all lived with him.

There was no doubt that Dobendu was a successful tailor. Dobendu had three sisters Ankeli, Athonia and Aggie. He also had several half-brothers. Okpato, Opuliche's grandfather had married many wives with the result that Dobendu had many half brothers.

Opuliche remembered her grandfather as a hairy old man who always sat on his reclining chair in the evenings tapping away at his snuffbox. He would inhale deeply from his snuffbox and stare dreamily into space. During such times, he forbade his wives to disturb him. Opuliche would peep at him from behind the door and wonder what he enjoyed in that dark brown powder.

Dobendu and Modiba were good Christians married in the Catholic Church. The marriage was well celebrated by their Christian brothers and sisters. It was a union that held many promises considering the family background of the couple. But Modiba did not get pregnant early as people had expected. This had worried Dobendu a little. But as a believer, he held that God would bless his marriage at His own best time. When all hope seemed lost, Modiba had become pregnant and the result was Opuliche. Although Dobendu would have preferred a baby boy as tradition expected, he was thankful that God had given him a child. Sometimes he would take the little girl along. His friends had protested but Dobendu would not mind them. He was taking his daughter to his workshop. Who were they to tell him what to do? Thus Opuliche would go abroad in Ahianwama town.

Ahianwama was several eighteen kilometres from Okiwe, the biggest town Opuliche ever saw as a child. It was there that her father had ordered special white foofoo for their meal. Opuliche had never seen white foo-foo before. She had compared it with the yellow and stale eba they used to eat at the village. In addition, the Onugbu that came with the foo-foo was sweet delicacy in her tongue.

There was another wonder for the little girl: eating from a table! To the little village girl, nothing could be so marvellous. Whether the table was small or big, high or low, such was never thought of in the village. There all the family sat on low kitchen stools. From there, they all dipped their fingers into the common soup pot. They would keep and eye on one another to watch any attempt to eat quicker than others or smartly drag some fish with the lump of foo-foo. However, in Ahiawana, Opuliche was eating on a table. She really could not forget that special life of eating alone by herself on a table.

2

Mother's Training

After Opuliche's birth, Dobendu and Modiba waited in vain for the arrival of another baby. The years passed rapidly and both parents doted on their daughter.. Yet, there was pressure on Dobendu to take another wife. As a Christian, he felt this would be going contrary to the tenets of his belief. Moreover, he loved his wife Modiba. So the couple persevered in prayer and gave their best to their only child Opuliche. Later Modiba adopted Felicia whose mother had died soon after delivery. Since Felicia was an offspring of one of her grandfather's wives, Opuliche found a half sister in Felicia. But this was not all. Modiba's benevolent spirit had several women sending their daughters to her for training in household duties. These girls also became her god-daughters. Through this way too, Opuliche had other 'sisters' living with her.

Opuliche was the only child, yet people were very surprised

at the resolute way in which Modiba insisted that Opuliche did the housework. There were those duties conventionally believed traditionally to be for women and those meant for men. Modiba did not believe that there were such divisions of labour in life. In addition to her own duties, Modiba also did those work normally believed to be exclusively a man's work: She used to change the thatch roof-mats of her house by herself. In addition, she would change the front-wall fronds when the old ones went bad. Dobendu, living 'abroad' at Ahiamwama near Okigwe had left Modiba saddled with these duties. Being hardworking, she did not want to trouble her husband with house work, as most women would have done. If she felt she could do them, she would do the work without any delay or complaint.

This outlook greatly influenced the young Opuliche who observed and emulated what her mother did. In several instances, Modiba would call on her to join her in these tasks. Many school children in those days did not do any farm work. In fact nobody would be so impudent as to send a whole school child to dirty her school hands in a common farm, which was considered a condescending work. But Modiba thought differently. She sought every opportunity to expose her child to the rudiments of farming because she believed that it was through hard work that one was able to feed generously.

One day, farm hands were hired to work on one of Modiba's large farms. They were digging the ground for cocoyam, and Modiba insisted that Opuliche must join these people to practise farm work. While digging, Opuliche had cut her big toe with the hoe and everyone stopped to help her get a timely first aid. They tied up the bleeding toe with some cloth and sighed mournfully at the size of the wound. They all wondered what Mama Modiba's (as they called Opuliche's mother) reaction would be when she saw the gaping hole on her only child's leg. A school child for that matter! Hoe cuts were grave accidents. Most victims might not recover from the infection that often followed. Hence in many places the offending hoe would be kept out of use for a long time.

Time had passed but Modiba did not show up at the farm. And Opuliche's toe was still bleeding. Therefore the other farm workers advised her to go home quickly so that she would not get more 'hoe cuts.' With the offending hoe already hung on tree in punishment, Opuliche, accompanied by a sympathiser, made her way home. Somehow the girl was grateful for the accident. This would teach her mother to send a schoolgirl to farm next time!

Along the way they met Modiba bringing food for the workers. Opuliche promptly doubled her crying. Se was now wailing louder and louder. And her sympathiser hissed and sighed in agreement. They made such a din that passers-by stopped to stare. Modiba seeing her child in the midst of such noise quickly came to the scene. Opuliche dramatically extended her wounded leg for Modiba's inspection. The mother quickly examined the leg and said words of pity. She then asked if the wound had been treated. The farm hand explained the first aid had rendered in the form of pouring urine on the wound and applying the juice of some herbs.

'Good,' said Modiba, 'both of you can now turn back to the farm and finish your work!'

Everyone stared at her in surprise.

'A wound from a hoe should not send anybody home from work,' she charged.

'But, but it is bleeding,' the farm hand ventured.

'The bleeding will soon stop,' Modiba countered. 'I believe you have had your rest Opuli. Now go back and finish up your work, because it is not good that one should quit work simply because of a hoe bruise or any slight injury for that matter.'

Opuliche, thoroughly downcast, was twice sorrowful when she saw her imagined rest from farm work vanishing in thin air with her mother's pronouncements. From that day, she learnt a lesson in determination. One day this would help her to bring her own children to be strong in character, and hardworking by nature.

Modiba kept a neat home. She was so neat that very early in life, Opuliche learnt how to keep herself and her environment clean. Modiba always insisted that Opuliche should tidy up and remove unsightly things! It didn't matter if the things to clean up were too dirty or messy. A day there was when Modiba and Opuliche were cleaning cocoyam together. Modiba had found her girl picking up the dirty cocoyam with extended fingers. Opuliche did not want the dirt in the cocoyam to touch her hand. Modiba observed Opuliche's face cringed in hard lines of distaste for being made to do such a laborious and dirty work. Quietly, Modiba left her own work and went over to her daughter. She put the entire gummy cocoyam dirt on Opuliche's two hands saying: 'This dirt will not stick to your hand, you know; you can always wash them later!'

Then she added what the little girl was never to forget all her life: 'Without these dirty hands how could you ever enjoy a dainty position in life?'

Indeed Modiba's dexterity at work made her a proud owner of seven farms. She worked consistently to maintain her farm since the opposite would have meant her losing the farmlands to some other greedy relatives. The village tradition stipulated that one became the owner of as many farmlands that one can cultivate. The hard working farmers were always richer than the lazy ones.

A Woman's Challenge

Although she worked hard at the farm Modiba would create some time in the evening for relaxation. During such times, she thrilled Opuliche to several captivating folk stories. She had a good voice for singing. Thus she would gather every one in the household for a rousing session of folk songs. Opuliche looked forward to these evening recreations when her mother would be less of the hard taskmaster and more of the loving mother with a tender voice.

On other rest days when Modiba was not at one of her numerous farms, she would take Opuliche to the compound for painting. She would make intricate patterns and designs on the mud walls of their house. This art was achieved by the use of native charcoal and red mud. From the hut they would moved to the outside walls and all the walls around the house. When they finished with the walls, Modiba would turn to her daughter. She would also draw varieties of curved and straight lines on the Opuliche's body by way of ceremonial body decorations with Nkasiana and Uli. After this, Modiba would adorn her daughter with beautiful waist-beads, hand bangles and necklaces of different colours and sizes. Later in the day Opuliche would pay several visits to her friends in the next compound so that they could admire her new outfit.

On a market day Modiba would rise early for work at the end of which she would carry her little wares including her hand sewing machine to the market. She sold little farm goods and used the sewing machine to repair clothes for people. Sometimes Opuliche would accompany her acting as her apprentice. Soon Modiba was to erect a bigger house to accommodate all her god-daughters and 'foster- daughters.' She worked so hard that many people came to depend on her, especially her husband's relatives. She did her best to satisfy them but they would never tire of suggesting to Dobendu to get another wife. Modiba knew of all these plans and suggestions. The thought made her very sad sometimes. But she took care to conceal her dissatisfaction.

Going to School

Opuliche went to school at a tender age. The zeal the mother had for Opuliche's education was so intense that Modiba sent her daughter to school very early in life. This was contrary to expectations. It was strange in those days to send children to school, especially female children. It was seen as a complete waste of money and human resources.

Opuliche found it so strange going to school. She would look longingly at her playmates as she passed by thinking why nobody bothered them with school. 'So why do my parents hate me so much as to send me to school? Why can't they leave me alone to play and wander in the bush like Rose and Nneka?' she fumed to one of her foster sisters who was seeing her off to school. Juli had no answer to her frustrated ranting. Opuliche therefore resolved to save the situation herself. As soon as the back of her usher was turned, she would make a detour from the school pathway to join the idle children playing and fooling around. She enjoyed these stolen hours so much that sometimes she would forget to return to school entirely. But reports soon got to Modiba concerning her daughter's behaviour. So she undertook to take Opuliche to school every day. Modiba would reach the school compound before going back home. That was how she ensured that the girl got to school. Nevertheless, it was not long before Modiba began to get tired of this morning routine. So the kind mother resorted to asking her daughter's teacher to write something on Opuliche's slate. This was to confirm that Opuliche actually attended school that day. The teacher readily complied. For fear of being discovered if she did not attend school, Opuliche endeavoured to be in school. But she hated every bit of the drudgery, she would tell herself.

One warm Saturday morning, Modiba mother as usual prepared some food for her and other items for school, and sent Opuliche out to school. That day Opuliche got to the school compound and there was nobody. She thought that she must have been too early. She complimented herself on her punctuality and wandered around the compound aimlessly. Soon the early morning fresh air and sunshine were beckoning her. She went under a tree to play. In fact Opuliche loved to and did enjoy playing very much. She soon lost herself in her own game. Much later the schoolteacher, Mr Alisai, came around to retrieve a book which he had left the previous day in his locker. He was surprised to see Opuliche properly dressed and her school bag hung around her neck.

'What are you doing here?' he queried the little girl.

'I have come to school,' Opuliche answered, hastily scrambling to her feet, and dusting her dress.

'School? Don't you know today is Saturday?'

'My mother said that I should come to school,' Opuliche quipped, wondering what was wrong with Saturday that people should not come to school on such days.

'Go home, there is no school today,' he said finally.

'Yes sir,' the little girl answered and waited.

Mr Alisai who had made to turn away was surprised to observe that his pupil was still standing at the same spot.

'Did you not hear what I said?'

The girl started in fear.

'I said go home,' the teacher was now moving in her direction. Opuliche backed away some distance and stood watching the teacher. Mr Alisai marched into his class and brandished his cane. 'Alright get home now or...,' he said finally.

The little girl had hid behind a tree to stare at the advancing the teacher. She crouched in fear as the towering figure stood before her. Opuliche began to cry. Mr Alisai was not used to his pupil behaving like this. He had always known Opuliche to be an obedient girl, although too playful some times.

'What is really the matter with you?' he now asked conciliatorily.

'It is my mother,' Opuliche whimpered. 'She will not be happy with me if I didn't go to school today.'

'But there is no school today, it is Saturday. Go home.'

'I can't go back. She will beat me if I don't show her the mark on my slate.'

'Oh, the mark on the slate, eh? Alright give me your slate.'

Opuliche happily handed over the slate to the teacher who took it into the classroom. He was out in a second. 'Here's your slate,' he announced, handing over the slate with chalk marks written all over it. Opuliche accepted it joyously.

'Thank you sir,' she beamed, turning away to fly away home.

'Wait,' said Mr Alisa. 'Take this too.'

The girl turned round and saw a brand new exercise book extended in her direction by the teacher. She stopped in her strides and looked at the smiling face of the teacher still extending the book to her. Then she grabbed the book and ran. 'Mama, come and see what I've brought from school today-o!' She was so excited that she forgot to thank the teacher. But the teacher understood Opuliche's childish state of mind. He rather laughed at her joy and excitement.

Opuliche was soon home to show the book to her mother. From that Saturday on, she never missed school. From that day too, the mother had no need to guide her to school any longer. She had changed instantly from a school hater to a school lover.

5

Modiba Passes On

When Opuliche was twelve years old, she succeeded in enrolling in St John's primary school, where she was doing her standard three. Although in a very far place, Opuliche used to walk it every day. By then, she had developed sufficient interest in academic work to brave the long distance. She was beginning to notice that her mother fell into bouts of sickness. When she queried her about them, she would reply it was nothing for her to worry about.

A few months later, Modiba became very sick. She complained of acute pains in her chest. Opuliche asked whether she should stay back and take care of Modiba, but her mother shooed her off to school.

One day, the pain was so much that large doses of Sloan's liniment was administered, but to no avail.

Ukwu, a respected dibia, was finally called in. He came wearing his goatskin bag and after due consultations with his cowries, he approached the bed of the sick woman and carefully felt underneath it. Slowly he extracted a bundle, which he exorcised with great vehemence. 'Some wicked person had tied Modiba's chest in that,' he announced grimly to the gathered assembly.

'Who could it be,' became the whispered questions. Everyone was beginning to give his neighbour a suspicious glance.

Finally Dibia Ukwu gave the offending little bundle to Isaac, a faithful apprentice of Dobendu, who also was present at the time. As Isaac went out holding the bundle with a stick, the native doctor let out three rounds of gunshot into the morning air. The shots were supposed to prevent Modiba from dying. But it startled the sleeping woman awake. She sent for her husband and requested everybody to leave the room. After a long time, Dobendu came out with a strained face. People wondered what must have gone on between the man and his wife.

Later that morning, around 10.00 a.m., Modiba quietly passed away.

Instantly screams of anguish and pain rent the air. One woman threw herself on the ground. It was Ohuka, her long time neighbour. Soon other women, in-laws, relations and friends joined. As the day wore on, other sympathisers came. In the crescendo of the noise, more people came to join the grieving people.

'What of Opuliche?' asked a voice. It was one of the new arrivals.

'That is true,' observed another, 'where is she?'

'Be calm, everyone!' rang a voice in the midst of the fear

and confusion. Every one turned to the speaker in surprise. It was Venni, Dobendu's elder brother.

He cleared his throat. 'My people I greet you all. A great tragedy has befallen us today. While we mourn the loss of our sister, we would not wish one corpse to grow into two.'

'What is he talking about?' interjected many voices.

He cleared his throat again and all became quiet. 'Our little daughter Opuliche is not yet back from school...'

'Ewuu-u-u'

'She travels far for her school. We will like some oil to put in her stomach before she becomes aware of her mother's condition.'

That was good talk, it was severally agreed.

'So let us all whisper together...'

With this announcement people mourned, but in a more quiet way.

Opuliche was on her way back from school when she met Mama Emeka, another neighbour hastening towards her. This was a few kilometres from their house. The woman seemed to be in a great hurry.

'Good afternoon Ma,' Opuliche saluted courteously.

'*Gudafun*, my daughter', she replied, passing her. Then she stopped abruptly. 'Eh hem, Opuliche, please have you seen Sunday?' meaning the boy who looked after her children.

'No,' Opuliche replied.

'Let me run back home bo-o, so that my children won't have to millipedes for lunch.' So saying the woman turned back in a greater hurry and sped off. 'Let Sunday continue running away from my home. He must come back someday, I know!' Mama Emeka said and as she ran so fast indeed she held her flapping breasts with her two bent hands her elbows sticking out at her sides.

Opuliche watched the young woman as she ran like three women in one. And she wondered why her children might have to eat millipedes for lunch. Little did she imagine that the whole story was made up for her sake. As she got nearer home, se noticed that more people quietly joined her. It was at the market square that she met her Auntie Mama Ankeliba. Opuliche was pleasantly surprised. Opuliche ran to embrace her then looked at her. The woman understood the unspoken question in the girl's eyes. 'Oh, the doctor asked for some things which I have come to bring,' came the ready reply from her aunt. When Opuliche heard this, she believed that the doctor was still administering treatment to her mother. She and Mama Ankeliba walked the last yards to the house.

When they got to the house, Opuliche saw some few people discussing away from the house. She greeted them. When she looked towards her mother's room, she saw more or less the same people that were there in the morning. Her Auntie then asked Opuliche to go, eat, and put away her school things.

She ate and drank to her fill. Then her Auntie conducted her to her mother's bedroom, where she lay in state. At the door of the room, the Auntie held back the anxious girl saying: 'Opuliche I have something to tell you, your mother...'

She never finished the sentence because Opuliche had already bounced into the room and seen her mother lying majestically in her wedding dress! The piercing scream she let out started another session of wailing in the compound.

Modiba had died on a Monday, but by next Wednesday, Opuliche was back on her way to school.

She would have loved to stay back at home to mourn her mother, but her father said that was the last request that her late mother made. Nothing should ever stop Opuliche from going to school.

6

The Road to Standard Six

Opuliche started high school early enough at twelve. She had had a good start at the primary level. Not that she could remember exactly when. She only knew that she used to go to school with Felicia her 'sister,' who was also her nurse. *Nnenne* Felicia would carry her on her back. The school in St. Patrick's Catholic Mission at Ikpeke was less than three kilometres from their home. Opuliche's main subject, as far as she could remember then, was to hunt grasshoppers with one boy Stephen of her age grade who was called 'Teacher' by every body.

When Opuliche did Infants I and II she was so young that she 'played' away the two years that both classes required. However she did remember being in Standard I. School to her then was a serious business. Their village school, which used to be a Standard Four school, was suddenly demoted to Infant school by the Voluntary Agency School Management. It cited inadequate number of pupils and non-payment of the required levy as reasons.

Opuliche in order to join Standard One had to live with the Onwubiko family in another village in Ogu called Umueleke. This was about twenty kilometres from her Ndudi home. She used to go home on Fridays to spend the weekend with her mother. Then she would go back to Umueleke very early every Monday. When Opuliche compared both homes, she found a lot of difference especially in feeding. Food was not a problem in Opuliche's home but here all the numerous children could barely feed at a meal. These adjustments were tough on young Opuliche. Thus she failed that year. The next year Opuliche had to repeat Standard One.

Meanwhile the school management had decided to restore only Standards One and Two to Opuliche's village school. Therefore Opuliche happily went to do these two classes from her dear Ndudi home, and so easily passed the years. The following year she was to go back to Umuduru in Oki division to do Standard Three. That was the fateful year of the death of Opuliche's mother.

Umuduru was about five to seven kilometres from Ndudi and with other four school children from Ndudi, she would walk the fifteen kilometres daily.

Opuliche had suffered a great shock at her mother's death in October of that year, but that mishap did not hamper her success at the December final examination. It was providence, she thought. And it was also her second mother: Mama Anthonia.

7

Mama Antoni

Mama Antoni had been living with the family as far as Opuliche could remember. That was ever since she had returned to live in her father's house after her marriage with her husband broke up.

When Mohiba was alive this Mama Antoni was the mother who actually petted Opuliche. She was always going to see why the child was crying, while her real mother, Mohiba, kept up with house duties. Opuliche used to sleep with Mama Antoni at times. She also developed the habit of always eating first in Mama Antoni's house before going to her own for more food. When her mother Modiba died, her father Dobendu and Mama Antoni were the only people who earnestly urged Opuliche to continue with her studies.

There was a day when Opuliche returned from her ten-kilometre school with tears in her eyes. She had been crying the whole way. Opuliche had come to tell the household her sad story on the way: She had had a tiff with a girl. In the course of their heated exchange of words, the girl had said Opuliche was happy by her mother's death, otherwise she wouldn't have been too eager to resume her studies. Too shocked by this accusation Opuliche had cried all the way home. After she had reported this with tears in her eyes Mama Antoni burst out in great vehemence, 'Even her own mother will die some day, and then she will understand the pain of losing a loved one.' Opuliche was relieved. She pulled down her breath in solace. The entire house cursed the girl Ekworo for saying such an abominable thing, especially, as she had been one of the late Mohiba's god-daughters.

There were many things Mama Antoni did to prove to be a worthy mother substitute. Two years after Mohiba's death, a suitor had written a letter to Opuliche, telling her to leave all about schooling and be ready to marry him: 'It is time for you to stop school, and go to serve my mother's kitchen' he wrote. The man was handsome and was called Igwenga Opobo. To leave home and 'live abroad' was one of the best ways of attracting a girl in marriage in those days.

Mama Antoni was furious when she learnt of the contents of the letter. 'Get paper and pen,' she commanded Opuliche. 'Write exactly what I will tell you! Tell him that although your mother is dead, your father is still living today! And he has not decided to stop you from going to school. So you will not go and serve in his mother's kitchen because you are still a school girl'! Igwenga was later to marry Okpoasi Ekworo. Mama Antoni was quite bemused to hear this.

8

Adazi Venture

After her mother's death, Opuliche was still walking the Umuduru road to read Standard Four. The next year, she was promoted to Standard Five class along with other pupils who passed. But this meant going to St. Phillip's Catholic School Akeme in Ogu. Akeme was about thirty-four kilos from Ndudi village. Opuliche had to live again in somebody's house to attend school as she did in her standard One. This time however, Opuliche was bigger. She lived with one Louisa Ogbo. Louisa was bigger and in Standard Six and he looked after her like his real younger sister.

At the end of the year, the girls were told to go to Adazi for the Entrance Examination to get into Girls' school for their Standard Six, there being no girls' schools around the Ogu area at the time. It was just a day to the examination. Opuliche was on her way to Adazi for the entrance examination. Isaac, one of her father's apprentices, was carrying her on a bicycle. Isaac was very tall, strong and good at cycling. But when Isaac and

Opuliche got to Osina, which was now ten kilometres from Ndudi the bicycle lost both its brake and bell.

There was not time for repairs. So they decided to manage on just like that. Later when they ran into a group of men who were telling stories with wild gesticulations, there was no warning bell ringing to alert the pedestrians. Before they knew it, they had crashed headlong into the men. Isaac injured his left hand. The bicycle was no longer in good riding condition after the accident. Opuliche and Isaac managed to drag it along until they reached the Orie market at Uga. Uga was Isaac's hometown. Isaac hired another rider to convey Opuliche to Adazi and stayed back at Uga to repair the bicycle.

The hired hand was good on wheels. He was riding with good speed to get his passenger to Adazi on time and also return to Uga that night. Nightfall saw them at the height of the steep Agulu hill which had a deep sandy bottom. They were now two kilometres to the convent. The man started descending the hill on speed. As they went down the hill, momentum seemed to gather of its own accord. Soon they were flying uncontrollably. The sandy bottom rose to meet them with a noise like a waterfall. Opuliche lost consciousness.

It was about nine o'clock the next day when Opuliche was conducted into the examination hall with bandages on her face. When she had encountered a second and more serious bicycle accident, some kind people had taken Opuliche, obviously badly wounded, to a hospital. There, the people learnt about her destination: that she was to take an Entrance Examination the next day at the college in the convent. Luckily the college was quite near the hospital. The nurses were so kind that Opuliche was able join others to write the papers on time. Before the examination, Isaac was waiting in the school compound ready to take Opuliche home. Opuliche was relieved to see him. She resented the rider of the previous night. Isaac's presence was so assuring that she finished the examination in great spirits.

9

Standard Six

The result of the final examination at Adazi showed that Opuliche was one of the two candidates from Ogu who passed. The other two girls who had written the examination did not pass.

The year that followed was one of indecision and dilemma in Opuliche's family. Everybody remembered the portentous accidents on the Adazi venture. It was enough to chill the blood. What sign could this be? they had wondered. It was too dangerous to go to that far-away Adazi after all these warnings. Moreover she was too small to go and cook for herself at Adazi. With no better advice Opuliche was to go and repeat Standard V at the nearest girl's school at Urua.

But Opuliche did go to repeat the class at Urua. A few days later she was forced to change her mind. The reason for that sudden change of mind might appear childish to a grown-up but it mattered very much to the little girl.

Opuliche happened to go with others in St. Bridget to Iyielle a spring near the Urua convent. The other 'children' were really adults. It was such a tug-of-war to fill one's bucket with water. There were many rude and rough people who quarrelled, pushed and fought just in order to fill their vessels. It was obvious to Opuliche that these people were accustomed to that rough business. And it scared her. Finally when she filled her own bucket it was even more dangerous to climb up the high uneven hill of Iyielle. She had barely reached the top of the hill when she slipped and fell. Opuliche nearly died from that nasty fall. As she rolled down the jagged hill, her bucket of water rolled with her in turn. The rough, tough students of the school had burst out in laughter and derision. Her misfortune was their source of exhilaration.

Opuliche was shocked by the whole experience, especially at the idea that the even her fellow girls had found delight in her misfortune. She was not used to this kind type of life. She made up her mind to go to Adazi and brave whatever may come out of the signs that the so-called double accident may portend. Moreover she will be starting a new class rather than repeat a class she had already passed along with some heartless fellows. She went home at once to her father Dobendu and told him of her decision. By Monday, the first day of the next week, Opuliche's father had made all the necessary arrangement to get her to Adazi.

People always wondered and queried why Dobendu should oblige a female child so much. Dobendu always abided by his child's decision in matters of education. Perhaps it was because of Mohiba's last wish coupled with Dobendu's vision to give his child a better education than he had. And despite the numerous hardships at Adazi, Opuliche patiently persevered. Moreover she was doing a whole standard six, and not repeating five, thus gaining a whole year.

Opuliche was not very good at cooking then. Every four days, from Ogu to Adazi, Dobendu would send some ready-made soup and foo-foo to her. There at Adazi, the pupils including Opuliche had to go to Ezu for water. Ezu was the stream that lay near the market. To get there one must run twenty kilometres through valleys and great hills on both sides of a rough and almost barren land. There were no houses. The place was a semi-desert filled with sandy red soil. This experience affected the night dreams of the young school girls who trotted there daily.

Adazi convent had two types of boarding pupils: the boarders who ate at the convent and those who cooked by themselves. This latter group was quartered at St. Bridget's hostel. This was where Opuliche lived. The girls in St. Bridget's house must run all the way to the stream and carry out other chores and must meet the evening class schedules in the convent. Opuliche began to look emaciated after some weeks. Many girls capitulated but she refused to give up.

'What's the cause for this sudden tallness of Opuliche's,' Mama Antoni asked one day as she observed Opuliche who had just returned from school.

Hunger and discomfort at the Adazi,' replied Dobendu, who had been to see her daughter several times at the convent and knew the aridity of the area.

The two different boarding scholars at the Adazi convent

had very few things in common. The boarders who were fed by the institution usually had their siesta while the St. Bridget's house girls who cooked for themselves usually ran along after dinner to get water from the far stream. St Bridget's House was provided so that poor parents who could not afford to pay for their children in the boarding section (a place with zinc house and cement beds) might at least afford to give their children some education. St. Bridget's girls usually pay lesser fees since they did their own cooking. They lived in thatched houses with mud-walls and mud-beds. Opuliche's former classmate Betina, the girl with whom she passed out from St Philip's school, was in the boarding section. The boarders naturally felt superior to the girls in St Bridget's house. Thus Betina and Opuliche rarely associated although they hailed from the same place.

That year's Standard Six examination result was not good at all. Many of the pupils failed. How they wept and bemoaned their bad luck! The successful ones were very and would not show much signs of joy until the ill-fated ones who failed had quickly taken their exit from the school. Away they went to complete their weeping in their fathers' houses and to receive a more sincere commiseration ('sorry') from their own people. How they wept broken-heartedly at the sight of their classmates who had passed! Opuliche remembered how one Beta Onya was knocking her head against a pillar when Opuliche and others went and said 'sorry' to her. She knocked her head to punish that 'her head' which had disappointed her in that year's Standard Six examination.

10

School Condo

Adazi was in an uproar because of the mass failure at the Standard Six examination. By 4.30 p.m. that Friday when the result was called the girls who failed had all left the compound in anger. Only the successful people were left in the convent. Banding together these girls danced, jumped, laughed and galloped with joy to celebrate their 'pass' result.

Opuliche had a friend at St. Bridget's called Celibret. Celibret had passed standard five while Opuliche passed six. Both girls went to Obi's Shade to buy things to eat and congratulate themselves for their success that day. Opuliche had a whole six-pence to spend.

Opuliche was determined to spend the whole money in her possession. Her father, she knew, would come with his bicycle the next day to take her home. She finished the whole sixpence in buying just rice, her favourite food.

It was a moon-lit night. The successful girls were almost wild under the moon light. No regrets! There was much merriment, singing and dancing in St. Bridget's house. Opuliche's favourite food was rice. And she had bought and cooked a pot full of rice. After some dancing with other girls, she would steal away from her group to scoop some spoonfuls of rice from the big pot she had prepared. She would put all into her eager mouth, swallow it and dance back to the other girls singing in the moon light.

Celibret was from Achina – a town on the same road to Opuliche's hometown. Opuliche was too excited. She could hardly wait in the school for her father to come for her. She decided to walk with Celibret some thirteen kilometres before they each would follow the different routes to their different homes. They had planned to carry plenty to eat on the way. Considering the long journey on foot Opuliche had cooked her whole rice. Their journey will start very early in the morning. The decision was good Opuliche thought, for if they remained in the compound, the Irish sisters might ask them to clean up the dormitory and the surroundings. Somehow something dreadful might even conspire to cancel this her successful result! She couldn't believe that she had actually passed a whole Standard Six.

Opuliche had had other considerations for joining Celibret to walk. She wanted to hasten the time when her father would hear the good news. 'O, My father will be so happy,' she gloated. 'And all the home people... yes even other people will hear it that I have passed!' Opuliche's head grew big with such thoughts. Before the cock could crow the next morning Celibret roused Opuliche. Gradually the cool gray light of morning brightened the horizon and more sounds multiplied. Opuliche and her friend put finishing touches to their luggage and after making sure that they did not leave any of their belongings behind set out on their very long and happy journey. The road was long but the girls were joyful and cheerful. It was not easy to pass the end of year examination. But they were cautious not to breathe too heavily or whisper a sound as they passed the school compound. They were apprehensive that the reverend sisters could give them work to do in the convent. These people could even cancel their good results on finding them making noise and leaving so early for home they told themselves. The two girls were behaving as if they were doing something wrong by going home early. Such was the terror in which the Irish sisters were held.

They were never told the reason for certain school disciplines like dumbness and quietness. That was how life used to be in the convent. In their minds there was confusion as to what was evil, what was bad, what was sinful or what was not. Little and improper understanding of the western lifestyle introduced by the sisters turned the convent girls into some kind of servile maidens. Everything was hidden without reason. 'Secrecy always' was the watch word.

But their fear had basis from what the girls could recall of some past happenings in the school. At the end of the last term some 'good' girls had gone to the sisters to enquire whether they could go home. But to their surprise the convent sisters had told these girls to remain behind and clean the compound.

The girls were bewildered at this unexpected injunction. The entire compound would be dusty and bushy by the time the school resumed for next term. As far as Opuliche was concerned these sisters would never show any joy or approval at the happiness of young people. So Adazi Holy Rosary School was a place where the unexpected was expected. It held the claim for being the right place for refining, reforming and training 'wild' girls who came from co-educational schools. Adazi was the only boarding primary school for only girls then. And it was religiously held that co-educational schools had bad, savage school boys and girls. The girls from such boys' school were made to believe that they were bad. The few girls who had been in the convent for some years often threatened the new boys' school girls with severe punishment from the sisters because of their rawness and lack of manners.

'You're very rude,' they would complain.

'You have no manners Opuliche,' the reformed, tame and polished girls would reprimand her. 'Can't you say please?'

Opuliche will hear this scolding ten times in an hour. She would watch the tame girls twist their mouths in distaste.

The tame and reformed girls after humiliating the new ones with work often resort to segregation. They would rebuke the new ones and show disapproval with their way of life. They would condemn, in their lofty Onitsha dialect, the 'boldness,' 'boyishness' and 'tomboy' manners of these unrefined new girls. Thus inferiority complex became the lot of the new girls from the 'wrong' school. They were said to be full of 'bad manners' which they exhibit by not saying with a bent neck and in meek voice: 'Thank you Miss' to a teacher who had given them an unjustified slap or whipping. In Opuliche's mind those teachers, prefects and 'old girls' were very wicked.

Despite these intimidations the new girls were sought out by the old maids and teachers who borrowed their books. Coming from a more challenged school, they usually had books which teachers in the convent schools never had. On fulfilling the request for such a book, woes betide any 'new girl' that would boldly say: 'Here is the book you requested from me'. That new girl must be punished for impolite expression. The new pupil with the head bent sideways, to show the existence of manners in her, should have said: 'Please Miss, this is the book.' The teachers of the time, in Opuliche's mind, were adepts at hiding their ignorance with fault-finding.

Once after school had closed for long vacation, a group of those 'goody goody' refined girls went up to the reverend sister in charge of the convent in voices that wavered uncertainly and necks that bent at an angle to show good manners. They also managed to produce artificial smiles on their worn and tired faces. Opuliche had followed them from a distance. She wanted to know how their mission would turn out.

'Please, Sister may we...' one of them started apprehensively.

'What?' interrupted Sister Mary Perpetua irritably. She was always busy and pretended not to hear. And they had told her again: 'Please sister... may ... may we go home now?' A bunch of fools in white dresses, Opuliche sneered at them from her safe distance. The school was officially closed, so why go to ask such a question? Opuliche wondered in righteous indignation as she watched the girls.

For a long time, there was silence. The busy reverend sister kept scribbling away in her book. It was as if she had forgotten the girls. Then remembering, she looked up and fixed them with cold steely eyes from beneath the rims of her eye-glasses. The air froze.

'Go? What do you mean by that?' she rebuked. 'No! You can't go,' she muttered. 'You must stay back and clean the school compound first!'

The good girls stood crestfallen. They were too timid to tell the sister that almost everyone was leaving. Cleaning the school compound by only such a handful of girls was work for several days. Opuliche was snickering as she sneaked away to tell her friend what had transpired. She was very happy that it so came out. The girls had done that only for what they called 'Condo.' One seeking condo usually pretended to be a very good girl just to impress her superiors. A girl usually seeks for condo so that she might appear special to other people, especially the authority.

The early-morning travellers had remembered the school condo incident and planned not to make any noise during their departure. They did not even wake up their friends to say goodbye of farewell to them. Celibret thought that the 'goodbye' they all said before going to bed was enough and Opuliche agreed. After they had passed the convent and the hospital compound Opuliche began to talk freely. But the cautious Celibret reminded her that it was not quite safe for them to talk yet until they had passed the reverend fathers' house. Didn't she know the fathers could report them to the sisters?

'They're all the same,' whispered Celibret. Opuliche agreed.

The girls passed the fathers' and doctor's houses and were about to pass the Church when they remembered that they should go in and thank God for so many things. There were very important things to thank God for. Number one of these things was: their pass result, and number two was even more important: their being able to leave the awful convent that day without being stopped and detained by the unpredictable school sisters.

11

Pot of Rice

Opuliche and Celibret did not stay in the church long, for their thoughts were focused on their homes. Soon they were ascending the long Adazi hill. This was the hill where Opuliche had had that terrible bicycle accident. It was good that after all she had boldly ignored the superstitious doubts in her mind and had decided to take on Adazi, otherwise her education would have suffered a year's setback.

Opuliche and her friend talked animatedly because they were now a safe distance from the convent and mission. They talked about their result, of certain friends whom they thought were very intelligent but who had failed. They planned how to tell all these to their people when they reached home.

After walking three kilometres, Opuliche told Celibret that they should stop and eat their rice. Celibret brought up another story about one girl in their class called Oriyido who used to impress people that she was very intelligent and came from a rich family. Both girls were happy at Oriyido's failure. They saw it as fitting punishment for all the lies that she told them.

'Yes, Oriyido is so boastful,' exclaimed Celibret. 'She had lied that her mother was a very rich woman.'

'Oh yes,' rejoined Opuliche, 'and not only that but that her father lived in a storey building with numerous servants.'

But all the lies came out in the open when her father visited the school unexpectedly one day. His buttocks were barely covered by the native 'pem-in-front and pem-behind' attire that he was wearing. This pant was called native 'pem-in-front and pem-behind' because of its ridiculously short and tiny size. To wear this attire, a man would tie a rope round the waist with a towel that barely managed to cover his private part. Both ends of the towel would dangle in the front and back of his laps. It was the attire of the poor set of people in those days.

'Oh, Oriyido is full of pretence,' the two girls laughed and laughed at the recollection.

The December air, the restful quiet, and the delight of the season's early sunshine had their effect on the joyful girls. But soon Opuliche was dragging her feet rather sullenly. Ironically she had grown less happy. Her steps continued to drag. She was walking far behind her friend Celibret. At last she could bear it no longer.

'Celibret didn't you hear my call?' Celibret was Opuliche's junior as she had only passed Standard Five while Opuliche passed Six. But now Celibret acted like she was in control of things. Actually she was older than Opuliche. 'Yes, I heard you Opuliche... but don't you think it is still too early to eat now'?

she countered, having guessed the reason for Opuliche's recalcitre.

'What time do you think it is now?' asked Opuliche.

'I don't know,' said Celibret, 'but all I know is that it is not yet time to eat.'

'Oh, my leg,' complained Opuliche.

'What's wrong with your leg?' asked Celibret, stopping.

'It is paining me so much. When do you say we shall rest, even if we were not to eat?'

'Very soon,' Celibret replied very much like a doting mother. Opuliche tried to fasten her mind on something like singing and recitation of poems but after some time, she lost interest in these.

The road they were marching on was neither even, nor straight. It would wound around from one end to the other, avoiding very deep valleys and some high hills. Had the road been straight, the journey would have been about four kilometres. The loneliness of the road made the girls' journey somehow irksome. After a very long silence, Opuliche again repeated her plea. This time she did not say: 'Celibret we must eat.' Instead she stated:'Celibret, any time you decide is right, we shall eat our rice.' Her tone was so full of resignation. Celibret observed that it was still not yet six in the morning and wondered why they should eat so early. Did not her friend know they had more than six hours of walking. She assured Opuliche that eating was better enjoyed after a great deal of hard work.

Opuliche continued to talk only and mainly about food and nothing more. She spoke of how they would sit for the meal by the side of the road. At a time she suggested to get water from people who were returning from their early morning stream --it was that early in the morning. The people of that area were used to going to stream from as early as three in the morning. Carrying their home made candles they would set out from their homes to go to the stream for water. Opuliche and Celibret met many of them going home from the stream. They were mostly women and children. Whenever one figure or more appeared in the distance, Opuliche would press on Celibret that they should stop the person for some water so that they could eat their meal there and be able to wash their pots with 'ready' water. On every occasion, Celibret would find some reason for canceling the idea and, like an elderly person, postpone the eating time.

At last, after nearly ten kilometres' of walking, Celibret agreed that they could now eat. The two girls got out their mats. They spread them by the side of the road. There was the level green grass with the sun casting a very lovely shade that bright December morning. The girls immediately felt at home. They felt more relieved when they set down their heavy loads. They quickly unpacked their things to get cups, spoons and plates and the food. A kind lady had given them some water with which to finish the meal. The people of that place, though they used to travel very far distance to get water, yet they never refused to give water to any traveler who asked them for some drinking water.

The two girls were very happy at their readiness for eating. Opuliche on her own part had made sure that she was as far from Celibret as possible. She believed that her own rice was much better to taste than Celibret's. Also she had greater quantity of rice. She did not want to share or give Celibret any bit from her pot of rice. It made a great sight therefore when she uncovered her pot of rice and found it empty.

'What am I seeing?' she exclaimed. 'Who has done this?'

Celibret was amazed to see Opuliche looking and talking like a mad girl. When she saw the empty pot of rice she burst out laughing so loud with her mouth full of her own rice. She had understood Opuliche's motives in setting her mat far away from her. A crowd had gathered to the scene because of Opuliche's bewildered gestures and shouting. 'What is the matter?' they asked.

'Who washed my pot so clean!?' Opuliche asked the crowd in consternation.

It seemed quite a mystery. And to Opuliche's benumbed and hungry mind, she couldn't imagine the person that had played the dirty trick on her. Celibret however invited her to share her own rice. The crowd soon dispersed when the two girls settled down to eat.

It was while she was eating Celibret's rice that it gradually dawned on her that she was the thief that had stolen her own rice! She recalled the time in the night when she had sleepily eaten all the rice and even washed the pot because she thought it expedient then. That night they had packed their little belongings carefully. Soon after the dancing the girls settled for a happy, excited night rest. The compound gradually grew quiet. They slept on the mud floor without a mat, cloth or blanket. They had all these items carefully packed away and not to be spoilt or rumpled.

After a while Opuliche began to feel hungry. Carefully, she got up from the bare mud bed, took some spoonful of her rice from the pot, and went back to bed. Other girls lying down on their own mud beds in the dormitory were sound asleep long ago and were probably enjoying beautiful dreams about their success. But the thought of her rice and imaginary hunger kept Opuliche awake. At sleeping intervals, she would get up from bed to eat some more of her rice. Then she would lie down. And up she got again, repeating the same procedure. The silent hostel bore witness as Opuliche took more and more spoons of rice and fell back on her mud bed. Although very groggy and half asleep, she still got up several times to scoop some more spoons of rice into her mouth. When the food remained very little she decided to finish it all. She sat up decidedly and ate up all the rice. Then quietly, she took some water and washed her pot very clean. She did not blame herself at all; after all, carrying a pot of rice would increase the weight of the already heavy luggage the next day. Again she reasoned that it would be difficult to wash the pots on the way, there being no river or stream to cross. Not until Opuliche had eaten up all the rice and had washed her pot did she sleep without further distraction.

After the meal, the two friends continued their journey with joy and further jokes. They sang songs and directed their strong feet in rhythmic beats. They walked past Ekwulobia, Aguata, and then to a very long hill after Isuofia. When they had descended the very long hill there was silence. The narrow path by the left side of this road meant very much to the two friends. It meant they must part ways. Celibret must go by the narrow path for it led to her own home in Achina.

Opuliche looked at the dull and lonely road that gloomily lay in front of her. Only her, all alone on that lonely road! After Celibret's departure and disappearance in that pathway, Opuliche knew what it meant to be left alone to herself. She stood on the spot looking emptily at the lonely and lengthy road. The December mist had dully darkened Opuliche's gloomy atmosphere. But then she remembered that the road led to the place where she was to announce her success among her people and took courage to walked on. This time, she was singing songs at random. She marched like she was half-mad, with her luggage on her head. Her long strides were careless, her free hand, swung at full length to the rhythm of the song that she happened to be singing at the time.

Ascending the Ayika hill Opuliche saw something like two dots in the very far distance. The road from this point was straight. They looked to her like two small cats sometimes running, and then walking. The cats soon became two dogs in Opuliche's eyes, gradually enlarging to look like two goats, this time, with two other little goats closely beside them. The scene appeared actually like two goats and their young ones as Opuliche took a closer look. She was hoping to meet a living thing at last. The lone traveler began another song. But her anxiety for home, heightened up by Celibret's departure, disturbed her singing. Then she wedged her forefinger between her teeth. There was her father! She could now see through the mist that the two 'goats' with their young ones were in reality her own father and her uncle Venni!

She had some surprise for them all right. The two men were

ascending the hill, walking and wheeling their bicycles. Opuliche had agreed with Celibret on a drama that they would, at first, put on a sulky look to suggest that they had an unfavorable result at the end of the year. When asked by their people if they passed they would say 'No.' Celibret told Opuliche that this was just to tease them a little. The initial pretence would show them what their parents would have done if they had actually failed like many others. Opuliche was getting ready for the drama as her people got nearer and nearer with each step she took.

She had been rehearsing over and over how to enact her imaginary failure. Opuliche remembered especially the casting down of the face and false tears. Opuliche got well prepared for the drama which would begin in about ninety seconds. By this time her uncle and father were only 100 yards away from her. She took the necessary first step to the acting but suddenly found herself practically flying into the arms of her father: 'Papa, I passed, I passed-o'. She was almost beside herself with excitement that she could not pronounce the words distinctly. Dobendu asked her again: 'Did you really pass?'

'Yes-o-o' she replied joyfully, jumping in the air and hugging the duo. Dobendu extricated himself from the arms of his daughter and started riding his bicycle in circles. He kept on round and round the road with both his hands in the air! Venni was all the while laughing happily. He gave Opuliche a very good hand-shake, and then turned his attention to the bicycle 'magician' Dobendu whom he started showering with praise names: Ifemelumma! Dike-eji-ejemba!

When Dobendu got over his excitement he asked his

daughter several questions concerning the school and her result to which he did not wait for any reply. He was beside himself with excitement. Venni packed Opuliche's luggage onto his bicycle while Dobendu rode off with his successful daughter as his passenger. The men sang, whistled, talked and laughed in uproarious ways. They threw loud greetings at anyone they met on their path.

Part Two

12

One in Town

The Christmas of that year was the happiest that Opuliche had known since her life. Many people came from far and near to see the girl who had passed standard six. She was the first girl to pass standard six in her local community. This attracted many rich suitors who came with cars to ask for the girl's hand in marriage. But what was her father's reply to them?

After breaking the customary kola and drinking the usual palm wine, Dobendu would address the suitors as follows: 'Well my dear ones, the girl is still a child; she is too young to marry now. *Book* is her husband for now. Please do not be offended. When she grows up and gets sufficient sense of her own, if she would like to marry, then she will have to look for somebody of her choice.' The guests would dust their back and walk uncertainly out of the obi.

Dobendu used to recite the above speech so frequently that relatives who viewed his ideas as ridiculous would help him out at times. 'Yes, *book* is marrying her for now,' they would conclude and snigger to themselves.

January came. Opuliche went to Adazi for teaching employment as a pupil teacher. Other colleagues of hers, Veronica, Catherine, Lucy and Cecilia were there too. Cecilia was closest to Opuliche because both were new teachers whereas the others were old in the system.

Soon at Adazi, their daily conversation used to be about when the 'pay-day' would come. 'Pay' referred to the stipend they received after deduction of feeding and lodging allowances. These young teachers never minded that they were fed and housed along with students. They were more intrigued by the idea of handling a chalk and controlling a class. Opuliche, despite her small size, was fascinated by the whole experience.

The first pay-day was not as wonderful as anticipated by the young girls for, in addition to deductions for feeding, part of the teachers' uniform bill was also deducted from that month's pay.. However, the young teachers did not mind this as long as it did not interfere with their sense of power. They assured themselves that it was better to stay on as teachers irrespective of their grade than become students again.

Reverend Sister Mary, the manager of the school, had repeatedly suggested to Opuliche to train in the Teacher Training College which lay in the next compound. However, Opuliche had not seen any need for further studies. After all, there was none like her in her town and a few yonder villages. Her people were never tired of reminding her of how special she was. They assured her that her achievement was spectacular. Her head had begun to swell with pride. She became happy and content. She became proud!

One Sunday evening while she was at home for a holiday, she decided to visit the village church. The church compound was also the school compound. A group of older boys was playing football on the field at the time. So all pedestrians made use of the narrow footpath that wove around the football field.

Opuliche finally came out of the church. She had on her new gown which showed off her fine slim figure. With her hands in her pockets, she surveyed the scene before her. Then she made up her mind. With her face turned up at 'a-quarter-to-ten' angle, she made for the centre of the field.

Opuliche did not look at anybody, for in her mind, those insignificant men playing ordinary football were not worth noticing. After all they had not passed standard six. As she passed through the field in her world of arrogance, the ball rolled on her legs. Without talking or changing the position of her head, she bent down in her most elegant convent manner and picked up the offending ball. She held it in her left hand. Of course, her right hand was still in her pocket. The game came to an abrupt interruption.

The players surrounded Opuliche. They teased her to release the ball. But it fell on deaf ears. Then Opuliche noticed some of these players. They were actually older than she was. In the past they were people that she used to show respect with loud greetings of 'good morning sir!' However, that was before. She had now passed her standard six. She was earning a salary.

She was now called 'Miss!'

She coolly surveyed the gathered crowd with an air of contempt and disdain. She had a steady snobbish gaze for each one of them. They had begun to shout and some mouthed abuses to make Opuliche throw back their ball but she did not move her lips in reply. Then she noticed Godrick. She used to respect the man. As she gazed at him steadily, the young man said: 'Opuliche throw down the ball now!'

Opuliche did not like the 'illiterate' way of pronouncing and calling her name. He could not even attempt to pronounce the name in Onitsha dialect, which was used by the few educated people then. Moreover, he had omitted the all-important title 'Miss.' Opuliche was piqued. '*Mgboo Godrick, kedu ife ina elo maka m?* she retorted,' meaning: 'You, tell me Godrick, don't you know who I am (that you dare talk to me with disrespect)?'

There was a hush. It was the voice of Opuliche at last. What a rude question, they wondered.

Godrick looked round; he looked up and down. The man was quite embarrassed both by the rude manner of address and the question itself. Everybody used to call him 'Goddy' out of respect, but here was this small girl calling him like his father would. He bit his lips. By then there were more church members turning into the field to find out what was amiss.

Godrick held Opuliche's gaze and roared: 'What I think is to slap-shut your eyes this minute!' His team hummed and murmured like a hive of bees. Then very placidly but rigidly, Opuliche turned her left cheek to Goddy and said in cold defiance 'Slap me then!'

Godrick raised his hands, but instead of delivering the

threat, he merely pushed the ball through the Opuliche's arm. Her head was still turned at angle 'eight-twenty.' The boys went running to retrieve their ball. The game of football resumed and the crowd quickly dispersed.

Opuliche went away from the field as slowly as she could. She never looking behind.

With so much pride in her head further reading was not easy for Opuliche to accomplish at this stage. The reverend sister made her suggestions several times. She really wanted Opuliche to go on to college but Opuliche would pout and say nothing. She would not talk until she had confided in her peers who would naturally talk her out of it since they had concluded then that going to college was a waste of time. They calculated that if they stayed on and got paid every month, why then should they bother to go to college? At other times Opuliche overheard Miss Onochie boasting that she would go to college only after she had taken the 'C' salary. So Opuliche made up her mind that she too would go to college only after taking the 'C' salary herself. But reverend sister Mary was persistent. She withdrew Opuliche from teaching in the class and kept her idle for several months. During this period she continued to feed the young girl with the idea of going to college. When this failed, Veronica deployed her to work in her office. As the school manager, she used to visit the out-stations with Opuliche. The reverend sister would also take Opuliche along when on supervision of those 'bush schools.' It was on one of these visits that Opuliche met her previous classmate Florence. Florence had read standard six with Opuliche at the Adazi primary school and had failed. Now she was repeating standard five.

While they were going back to the convent, as usual sister Mary spoke to Opuliche again about getting into the college. But while the sister talked, Opuliche marvelled at her own unique position in life. Seeing Florence in ordinary primary five made her feel she was doubly successful. She was too happy and content with her present station in life to worry about any college.

When sister Mary 'disturbed' her about going to college again, Opuliche told the reverend sister that her father had no money to train her in a college. No problem, said sister Mary. She would arrange for the fees to be paid by the school. Later Opuliche could pay back the money in monthly instalments after she had graduated from college and was teaching. 'Some bright students have been so sponsored,' the sister explained to her. 'Now go and discuss this with your father.'

Instead of going home immediately, Opuliche once again went to consult her peers.

'You will have no voice in that college!' one said.

'Ha! ha!' they laughed. 'The students will be calling you 'P.B.'

'What is that?' asked Opuliche.

'Pay back!' they explained doubling in laughter.

This was the laughter and the mockery of the very inexperienced but harmful group of teachers in Opuliche's gang. With such derision Opuliche went home and never discussed the issue with her father. She came back the next day to the reverend sister and said: 'My father said that I must never get into a college.' The reverend sister was so infuriated by the answer that she returned the recalcitrant Opuliche to her class immediately. That should put an end to this meddlesome interference in her affairs, Opuliche thought happily.

13

Tragic July

Dobendu had very patiently waited for another child by Mohiba. But this was not to be. Friends and relations had prevailed on him to marry another wife. But Dobendu was never tired of reminding them that he was a Christian. However, at a time, the power of their advice and remonstration of relations began to outweigh other 'church considerations!' Dobendu married Ubani as a second wife. This was some few years before Mohiba's death.

But soon after Mohiba's death poor Ubani was sent packing. What happened? It was discovered that she could not wait to seize the deceased first wife's wedding ring for her own. She had impudently put it on her own wedding finger. Dobendu took astonishing exception to that. He quickly put her things together and sent her home to parents. Opuliche was happy at the rejection of Ubani for she never liked her. With Ubani gone Dobendu had to stay until four years after his wife's death before he made up his mind to marry again. This time he married Mary-Rose. The marriage was solemnised in the church in April. On May 9, the first issue from this marriage celebrated. It was another female!

That year was also another year of death in the family. After the death of her mother Mohiba, Mama Antoni had become her foster mother taking care of Opuliche's welfare as much as she could. Mama Antoni's main occupation was trading. She traded in delicious dry asa fish. Opuliche used to eat from some of the woman's big basket of dried fish for sale and the woman never complained. In fact Mama Antoni seized the opportunity of Mohiba's death to pamper Opuliche. And the latter loved her dearly.

At this time Opuliche was a first year pupil-teacher in Adazi Holy Rosary School. Dobendu had just married his wife Mary-Rose. It was barely six days after her brother's third marriage that Mama Antoni died. Opuliche was at school then. It was there at Adazi that the messenger came to bring her the sad news.

'Mama Antoni is dead?' she queried stupidly.

'Yes, she died barely six days after your father's wedding,' was the answer.

Opuliche broke down and wept. Accompanied by the messengers she went to the reverend sister in charge to obtain permission for her travel. But the sister refused her to leave the compound before the school was over. Cajetan and Nwagu the two messengers stared in surprise. 'But these are women who should understand what it means to lose someone,' Cajetan fumed.

'Their hearts must be dead-white the way their bodies look,' replied Nwagu with feeling. The two men hissed and went back to their bicycles in frustration. They tried their best to console the weeping Opuliche who felt more broken hearted at the stiff front of the reverend sister. The two men had been sent with two bicycles to collect Opuliche from Adazi. But they went back to Ogu without Opuliche.

After the school had vacated, Opuliche set out on foot for her lonely journey home. She had to cover over fifty kilometres on foot. She was singing all the funeral songs she knew as she trekked the lonely miles. Sometimes she trotted. When she grew tired, she walked. By the time she got home, Opuliche was so tired that she did not cry much. She merely asked, 'Did Mama see a reverend father before she died?'

'Yes,' answered her uncle, 'the Reverend Father Martin came and gave her the last sacrament.'

Opuliche was happy by this revelation. She said to the people: 'Why do you cry when our own person is now in heaven?' Such had been the power of the doctrine that Opuliche got from the Church. Her words had the effect of calming the mourners. She comforted the rest of her family as the enlightened one among them. Dobendu was really proud of his daughter's progress.

After the burial of Mama Anthonia, Opuliche went back to her station at Adazi. On July 15th Opuliche and other girls were preparing for evening benediction, when reverend sister Mary walked up to her.

'I have a message for you,' she said beckoning to Opuliche to come closer.

'We just received a message some minutes ago that your father is dead.'

Opuliche stared at her in disbelief.

'Your people are at the gate waiting for you,' she added and moved away. Opuliche continued staring at the straight retreating back of the white sister. The next second she was racing to the gate with great speed, and hoping all the while that there must have been a mistake. Was it not Papa that she saw a few days ago when she went home for Mama Antoni's burial?

Truly, her people were the gathering shadows that she saw at the gate. Their silence confirmed the reverend sister's story. Opuliche broke down and cried.

This time the school management allowed Opuliche to travel home with the instruction that she must return to school the next day. She prepared her things quickly. She came back to the gate in silence and followed her people to Ogu. They went on two bicycles. Opuliche was with John Ume on one bicycle, while the other man took her belongings and cycled alone. On the way, Opuliche was saying some prayers in her mind. 'To the soul of the faithful departed eternal rest grant oh Lord...'

Often she would wonder about the reverend sisters and their brusque manner of breaking sensitive news. How could the death of a beloved one be pronounced shorn of all sympathy. Such blunt insensitivity was quite unlike her people's thoughtful manner of conveying tragic messages.

They had not travelled about four kilometres when it began

to rain. It rained so bitterly. It made that day always very fresh in Opuliche's memory. 'Where did Papa die?' she enquired of her people amidst the rain, then remembering the church's advice on prayer, Opuliche wanted to know whether her father saw a priest before his death.

'Yes,' they promptly told her.

The men were a little surprised at this mood of affableness. Encouraged by the brave way she had taken the loss of her father, they proceeded to give her details of his ill health and battle with malaria. The men later confessed that Opuliche's peculiar courage gave them very great relief. They had been wondering how to broach the subject, but they saw that there was no need to hide anything from her. They had planned to deceive Opuliche by telling her that her father was sick and had told the reverend sister the truth so that Opuliche could be allowed to go with them. They never dreamt that the white sister would divulge the bad news to Opuliche so thoughtlessly. The men told Opuliche how her father had been taken to the hospital at Okigwe and how the reverend fathers and sisters had visited him regularly. He had not asked, so was not told, the special attention given to him by these reverend gentlemen was because they knew that he would soon die. When they gave him the last sacraments the doctors advised his people to take him home.

The travellers reached home rather early in spite of the time they left Adazi. Immediately they got to their compound, Opuliche jumped down from the bicycle and ran into the sitting room. She expected to see her father lying in state. She ran from room to room, searching, but all she saw were empty beds. She then ran out to the little group of people gathered outside the house who were her relatives. They understood the question in her eyes. One of them pointed to the fresh mound of earth in front of the compound. She stared at the mound and the people in disbelief.

'How could they?'

She wandered about dumb with shock.

'How dared they?'

She opened her mouth several times but no sound came out. She kept staring at them stupidly. So after all the haste her father had been buried before she could arrive. She did not see her father's body.

The relations gave many reasons for burying him before her arrival. The most cogent, they said, was the threatening rain. They wanted to bury him before the rain. Opuliche listened but never understood any of these reasons. As far as she was concerned, it was because she was a girl that made her presence in the funeral inconsequential. But they never knew what her father meant to her.

Blinded with fury, agony and desperation, Opuliche ran to the grave. She was soon busy vigorously uncovering the grave. She meant to take off all the sand.

'I must have a glimpse of my father!' she moaned piteously as she went about her task. No one could stop her. Not even some big, tall and huge men who pulled their shirts sleeves in an attempt to carry her away from the grave. They soon found that they could not. She fell from their shoulders several times as she made desperate attempts to get back to the grave. She clawed and bit until finally they let her alone. She went back to the grave and continued with her work of unearthing her father's coffin. The people looked on in disbelief. They had never witnessed such display of strength from a woman before. The men were afraid to get close to her as she had laid waste all their previous effort.

It was at this point that Mama Angelina, Dobendu's remaining sister, approached Opuliche and touched her gently on the shoulder. She quietly explained that Dobendu's burial was not done to slight her. The approaching rain hastened their action. Moreover, they had wanted to cement the grave. Mama Angeliba told her that the grave would be cemented on time and that was why they buried Dobendu in the frontage. Otherwise, he should have been buried in his own room which was rather the custom of the people. It was considered an honour to be buried in one's own house. Her calm voice had a ring of truth to it. Opuliche's hands slackened in mid-action, then stopped. She slowly stood up and left the grave totally deflated and went in to have a good cry.

The next day, Opuliche was taken back to the college.

Adazi gave her enough quietude to think over her solitary life. She had been an only child. There were no brothers or sisters and now, she was among other things, a complete orphan! She sought solace in the Christian doctrine and some other activities of the college.

The tranquillity Opuliche enjoyed in the college compound was to be interrupted by the midyear holidays. Then for the first time, she thought of where to go, with whom to stay, and who will take her back to the college. The financial aspect of it all was what bothered Opuliche very much. She and her father had jointly paid the fees of the first year, but what of the payment for the second year? The traditional custom of inheritance in Opuliche's locality did not help matters. Tradition had it that without a male child, the property of a deceased person would not go to the wife or female children of the dead man, but to the next living male relative. This next male relation could be an extended and far away uncle. Of course, in practice things could be modified if the new heir did not intend to be wicked. But Opuliche was not too lucky.

The next male in the compound was an uncle, who took custody of Dobendu's possessions. He took everything and left nothing. On the issue of Opuliche's education, he told her to go and marry. Opuliche saw her academic ambition coming to a sudden end. In great sorrow, she ran to her aunt for consolation.

Mama Angelina remembered one Nwankwo living in Enugu. He was reputed to be one of the richest men in Ndudi. She dictated the words while Opuliche wrote. They told him that Dobendu, his brother had died, leaving everything uncompleted. The most heart-rending of all was the child stranded at Adazi teacher training college...

Nwankwo was a kind man and lent money to pay the second year's school fees. Thus even before the school year started, Opuliche was the first to pay the school fees for the year. When Opuliche finished from the college and worked, she repaid this loan with gratitude.

14

A Sore on the Leg

Opuliche really enjoyed her probationary teaching years, with plenty of plaiting, love songs from record songbooks, imaginary love affairs and love stories that never happened in her life, but which she retold the other girls. The other girls in their turn did manufacture similar tales, and told them with such delightful accuracy that many, including Opuliche herself, were deceived that they were true life accounts.

The pastime continued until February when the indigenous reverend sisters at Urua sent Opuliche to teach in the area. The convent authorities must have considered that it was better for young girls to teach near their places of origin. Opuliche was hence stationed at a convent school in her hometown, in the village called Oyoma.

Almost as soon as she got there, she became very ill with a painful sore on her right leg. Opuliche could not remember what caused the wound but she knew that there were no antibiotics of any type that could be used on the sore. For treatment she was using some local red powder used to paint the face and to dye raffia palms for making local hand bags and table mats. Some young teachers were also using this red powder to beautify their feet. This powder was the only antidote that Opuliche was rubbing on the wound.

Instead of getting better, the sore got worse. She went to a doctor Igwebe. She was an elderly, kind and sympathetic woman. Opuliche had to leave the convent to live with Igwebe's family while taking treatment. Igwebe would wash the sore twice a day with some medicinal leaves. But each passing day, the sore on the leg became deep and septic. People used to cover their noses to enter the compound. It was said that Opuliche's nerves were beginning to show. Opuliche had stopped going to school. However, there was nobody to tell her school authorities of her health condition. They were considering sacking her for truancy. Ekworo, one of Modiba's goddaughters, was also teaching under the reverend sister in this girls' school. So Opuliche was no longer the only 'one in town.' Due to an earlier misunderstanding, Opuliche and the girl was not as close as they should be. Although the girl was aware of Opuliche's condition, she never intimated the reverend authorities about it.

Opuliche, on her part, did not bring any doctor's certificate for there was no nearby hospital during this period. In her ignorance, she simply assumed that the reverend sisters would get to know and pity her condition. She was expecting compassion and nothing more. She did not even know that she should write a letter to inform the authorities of her bad health.

One day Ekworo paid her a visit. Standing over the sick Opuliche she announced that she was sent to inform her that the school authorities were terminating her appointment. They had sent her to tell Opuliche to report to school immediately. Opuliche, lying on the mud bed with that her right leg up in the air, was still thinking of an appropriate reply to the message when the messenger walked out. Opuliche felt very sorry for herself on that very Sunday evening. But she was too hurt to act. Soon the letter of termination of appointment arrived. That even hurt more. Upon advice, Opuliche had to put that right foot on the ground. And walk to Urua she did!

At the convent, the manager, the reverend mother De Lourdes, saw the leg which was still dripping blood and was moved to sympathy. She gave Opuliche a letter with which to go on transfer to Emekuku convent. The pain on the leg could not allow her to get to Emekuku immediately. However, she was able to get some injections on the sore and, with time, the sore healed. Opuliche went to her doctor to thank them all. She also collected the rest of her cooking utensils still left at Ogu convent and headed for Emekuku.

On arrival at Emekuku, she was told that she reported too late since there was no longer a vacant class that she could teach. 'Proceed to Onitsha,' she was told.

At the Onitsha school the class teacher did not want to release her class to Opuliche. She was a 'C' teacher! A whole 'C' teacher while Opuliche was a 'P' teacher. Oh yes, the 'C' teachers then were a very strong and powerful set. This teacher should have gone on transfer to another school but she refused to go. She and Opuliche were teaching the some class at the same time! After two weeks, the daily drama of two teachers in one class was over. Opuliche was asked to go on transfer to Gboko in northern Nigeria.

15

Gboko

At Gboko, Opuliche found a companion in Miss Rose Okoli. Rose hailed from Onitsha. Other teachers there appeared too 'worldly wise.' So Rose had requested the Mother Vicar to send her another lady teacher to live with. The Mother Vicar at Onitsha was in charge of all the convent schools in the country. Gboko was, perhaps, a divine plan for Opuliche because it was there that she met Rose Okoli who introduced the delinquent Opuliche to a love for reading and all that could be termed virtuous. She was almost like a saviour in Opuliche's life being a college-trained teacher who loved reading. Thus with Miss Okoli's influence, Opuliche was reading a book a week. She had no time for plaiting hair and telling love stories. Those activities had taken her time at Adazi and Onyoma before her illness. Now she had to shave the whole hair off her head by herself. Her head was now as clean as a well-brushed coconut. That was the end of plaiting for Opuliche.

Rose took very good care of Opuliche's feeding and many other personal necessities for which Opuliche did not have to use her salary to acquire. The two girls acted like real convent girls in Gboko at the time with their pride and aloof sense of discrimination.

One night Opuliche was pushed to reproach a male teacher who had indicated an interest in her.

The man, 'Kakwuu' they nicknamed him, was a teacher on the staff of the Catholic School. The school was a mixed school and Opuliche really liked the competitive atmosphere. This male teacher was interested in Opuliche. He wrote her a letter to say so. He even started the letter with 'My dear sweetheart...' Opuliche was very angry. She went to the teacher's room to rebuke him.

'Who is your dear sweet heart?' Opuliche bellowed. Kakwuu was leaning on the table with his head bent down. 'I know,' was is dumb reply. Opuliche continued to roar like a wounded lioness. But the young man kept his head low with a small smile playing on his lips. To all her queries, he had the stupid answer 'I know,' which enraged the girl further. She put a finger on his forehead to raise his head up. But Kakwuu kept his head low.

Earlier, this male teacher had brought Opuliche some gifts. Every time people gave them gifts, Rose and Opuliche would empty the gifts in a pit behind their kitchen. They never took any gift from any man into their mouth. They were afraid that the men could influence their minds through these gifts. Even tins of milk or other canned food were deposited in the same place. Kakwuu's case was rather pathetic. To make sure that they did not like the teacher, they made up a name for him.

They gave him the name nkakwu which they modified to kakwuu.

The girls' attitude made men keep away from them. And they actually concentrated on their books.

Earlier at Gboko, Opuliche had applied for entrance examination to colleges. She received no reply. Her stay at Gboko was only six months. But it was a decisive six months for Opuliche. She had seen the benefit of education.

16

Holy Nweje Girls

The influence of church doctrine made the girls develop the holier-than-thou attitude which the men called 'holy nweje.' Many of the young girls believed that they were good only if they did not welcome men or boys. Only bad girls welcomed and entertained male company, they were told several times. Hence it was not strange that the female teachers were not married. The girls saw it as an ideal state for any good girl. Any association with men then in the training school was looked upon as not virtuous. You were a good girl if you were rude and unkind to the man who approached you. That man who showed any interest in you must be disgraced before people. Thus you became a good holy nweje girl.

All such trained holy nweje girls believed that they were being very good by their kind of life. It was a very rigid and proud life, and they called it 'to be intact.' In fact, many of these holy nweje girls stayed intact, as they called it, keeping to themselves till they finished all their studies. This helped them become single-minded in their studies.

However, many of these misguided girls were too rigid that they became lonely old maids in later life. Of course they despised men and everything that had any connection with men all the more. It was quite sad after all, for a child brought pride as much as the woman longed to be called 'Mrs. So and so' at certain age. This convent type of celibacy was brought from outside Africa. It was a strange notion that bred many desperate and unhappy women. At the end those relatives that she had trained usually despised the 'holy nweje' girl. They would even make fun of her single status. They would shun her in her old age. At this point, the holy nweje girl could be any thing but happy. Children were so important in the life of the average woman that a woman could be mother of her children without being married. However, Holy Nweje wouldn't know until they got to the dead end. What a fix for the proud, good and holy nweje girl!

One day, Opuliche, dressed in her immaculate holy white, had found herself in a big haste. She saw an approaching car and condescended to wave for a lift. The driver man drove past for a while and stopped, then reversed his car. When he drew alongside Opuliche he brought out his head and said: 'I do not carry holy nweje girls in my car!' The man made to drive off then relented and opened the door. He gave Opuliche a lift in his car quite all right, but Opuliche never forgot this incident and statement.

Holy nweje girls, the most sanctimonious people to meet, were not a likeable set afterall!

95

17

Sacred Snake

Eke was a sacred snake worshiped by the people of Nnobi. Irrespective of religious inclination, it was believed that everybody from Nnobi revered this snake. In Nnobi and surrounding areas, it was an abomination to kill the sacred python.

Opuliche and the other girls from the convent were sent to the school at Nnobi for their teaching practice. The holy nweje religious indoctrination included the idea that the downfall of man was as a result of the temptation of Eve by the devil who had taken the form of a snake. Snakes were therefore incarnations of the devil. The girls had been led to believe that if anybody killed a snake, she would get an indulgence for her sins. That was to say that any type suffering for her sins in this life, and even the next, would be waived for her. Since this idea took root in the Biblical account that Satan took the form of snake to tempt and to deceive Adam and Eve and consequently offended God, so any holy nweje girl who had the opportunity to kill a snake counted herself very fortunate and blessed. She would kill the snake with all the energy in her holy nweje hands.

One cool evening, Opuliche had finished her blackboard preparation for the next day's teaching. She had also helped other students her friends to prepare theirs. In fact, Opuliche was so artistic that in the college she did her blackboard preparation very well and very quickly. After these, Opuliche went from their senior primary section to the junior section to see other group of girls. The church was used as part of the junior section. As she walked into the big church and headed for the altar, she saw some girls shouting and pointing desperately. There, by the altar was a big snake! The snake was quite relaxed and not at all afraid. This increased their shouts. They were all badly scared. But Opuliche quickly jumped to the altar with another girl who was less afraid. With heavy sticks, they beat the snake to pulp and threw its body out of the holy church of God. The girls forgot all about the snake. They were feeling religiously happy that they had done very well. They were expecting lots praise and congratulations when the reverend sisters would hear of the incident.

Early the next morning however, many old women and old men came into the school. The time was about seven thirty in the morning. They were all carrying their own seats: showing that they had come for a long parley and were not at all in a hurry. As they arrived, they sat down in the big church field. In a short time, the whole field was filled up with people sitting very quietly. There was no talking. All the people were meditative, sad and with their hands by their jaws. Not even a whisper was heard by anyone passing. All the students looked on in awe. Soon a solemn group approached. The four old people requested an interview. The reverend sister in charge of the students came out herself and called Opuliche out into the field. Light-heartedly, Opuliche came out from her class with a chalk in her hand.

'Did you kill a snake at the altar yesterday?' one of the old women asked.

'What about it?' Opuliche rejoined carelessly.

'No, my child, do not talk like that,' one cautioned.

'Knock off the insult from that her mouth!,' came the shout from the back as one old man reached for her, but she instinctively went behind the reverend sister.

More threats rumbled around them: 'We will chop off her head with our knives!'

'Bring her here! Let her lie down here!

'Make her kneel down.'

The angry threats continued: 'Tie her up'!

'Shave off the hair from her head!'

The crowd was very much alive with agitation. While some shouted in anger others cried and gnashed their teeth in sorrow. Demands were heard from the injured and provoked crowd. Demand for vengeance and justice. Then the drum, the gong and ekwe started reverberating with deafening rapidity. Their solemn tunes told people that an important personality had died. Passers-by stood still in black dresses and held mourning staff in their hands. There was no market or farm work that day. Their mother had been murdered by a stranger. A tragedy has befallen them indeed.

Soon a large coffin was bought to the field *fully* decorated. The remains of the snake were carefully picked up and put in the coffin. They used leaves of palm-trees and akoro grass in making wreaths. Feathers from recently killed fowls were also added to the decoration. All these were put together to make quite a hideous decoration by the devoted villagers. Opuliche was made to kneel down under the great heat of the sun by the coffin.

Eventually Opuliche was convinced that she had broken a sacred law. At least the reverend sister had said so, as she tearfully pleaded for Opuliche's release. Seeing the sister weeping, instead of challenging the villagers, assured Opuliche that she had done a grievous thing. She was surprised by this strange turn of events. A reverend sister crying and pleading instead of being angry and telling the people that the snake had desecrated the altar. Perhaps she was wrong after all. She did wrong in killing the snake.

She began to cry. When Opuliche cried, the tears burst freely flowing down her chest in deep gasps. Her agony was quite intense. The leader of the women then asked her to come out from the sun. Opuliche paid no heed.

'Child, do you know has just spoken to you? Do kneel out from the sun at once,' a voice rang out from the group. Opuliche cleaned her eyes. It was the leader of the entire clan. Opuliche courteously thanked her.

Opuliche's life was spared. They did not shave the hair off her head as should have been done according to tradition. A teacher in the village who killed a similar snake was cleanly shaved. He died soon after. If this were not done the whole people, it was believed that all in the town would suffer greatly. After long consultations and debates, it was agreed that Opuliche acted in ignorance ad so should not be harmed. Some sacrifice however must be offered. It was a great concession for Opuliche.

The people were not telling lies. Rose, who helped Opuliche to kill the snake, had since taken seriously ill. She had large boils all over her body. She should have known about the sacred snake having hailed from Nnewi where the people also revered such sacred snakes. That morning she could not even come out of bed. Opuliche hailed from Ogu. She had told the people that Ogu people had no such custom or tradition. They did not revere the snake. She had killed the eke thinking that it was a mere snake not knowing its prestige in the town. Some people who spoke for Opuliche surmised that had the child been truly guilty, she should have been sick and suffering as Rose Okeke.

At last the sacrifice was made that very day. As a concession, it was in cash. The items for the sacrifice were calculated and shared among the two girls. Since neither of them had that kind of money, the pupils of the school quickly contributed and the money was paid. The people went and purchased the items and the funeral of the snake was duly observed.

Interestingly after this incident Opuliche became popular among the women of Nnobi. They showered Opuliche with gifts whenever she went to the market. These gifts ranged from kind words to items like coconut, pears, and oil-bean wraps. Opuliche was deeply touched.

18

Colonial Mission Teacher

From the elementary training college, Opuliche was posted to Awka-Etiti school. She set out with her little stepsister Betina.

It was a hectic journey.

The strange environment and rough roads did not make the journey any easier. At a point, there was no road and Opuliche had to come down and do the rest of the distance on foot with Betina on her back.

Finally, she arrived at the school with great relief. She was happy to meet the school head at the gate. Upon introducing herself, the head teacher said she had been asked to report to Dunukofia instead.

'What?' Opuliche blurted with shock.

'The letter to that effect was sent to you some days ago,' the head teacher explained.

'Letter? But I didn't get any letter,' Opuliche insisted.

'Well, it was sent. You are expected to report to Dunukofia immediately.'

Opuliche was crestfallen. What inconvenience! Especially to one who was so inexperienced about dangerous road travels. Worse still, this was the first year after training. She had no salary. But what did the administrator's care about the welfare of their staff? Anyhow, Dunukofia must be reached even if it meant carrying two-year old Betina on her back again.

Opuliche turned back to resume the journey and saw the uneven rough track practically staring back at her. She was disheartened. She remembered the long distance she had just trekked to get to her present location. Finally, Opuliche got a wooden two-wheel truck. The truck pusher was not a bad man at all. The luggage, including little Betina, were all safe inside the truck till they reached Nnewi. Conversations then were the only device to lull the tedious journey. So Opuliche tried to converse with the truck man. After all, conversation helped to ease the laden mind.

At last Opuliche got to Dunukofia. She was assigned to teach class two infants. She was happy to decorate the wall of the classroom with colourful drawings. Her class black board was daily decorated and made ready for teaching. She found to her delight several fruit trees on the compound. There were plenty of paw-paw, mango and different trees with many fruits. Given to drawing by nature, the trees made interesting drawing objects. A priest lived very near the school and they consulted him on their spiritual needs. Opuliche with others attended morning mass and other church observances.

In a few minutes, she was once more the happy woman she had always been.

There was a boys' school nearby. Opuliche liked this very much, maybe due to the intellectual stagnancy of the female Adazi environment as contrasted with the mental and moral liveliness of Gboko co-educational surrounding. Opuliche had at this early time displayed a preference for co-educational schools. She imagined herself once again reading and exchanging views with male teachers as she had done at Gboko. She had greatly enjoyed the experience then. During the teachers' conferences, the atmosphere was not dull. Discussions were lively and educating. People spoke on issues, ideas and concepts that she found challenging. She preferred this to the petty gossips that were the stock-in-trade of most female teachers in the convent schools.

This joy was not to last long however.

On the tenth day of Opuliche's arrival at Dunukofia, the manager of school, Reverend Ursula, came. She was looking for a teacher fresh from college called Opuliche Okpato. Opuliche was told to take a vehicle to Emekuku Elementary Training College. That was to be her new duty post.

'Just like that!' Opuliche thought bitterly. When she was beginning to settle down here in Dunukofia! What of her new made friends? What of her domestic problems? What of the distance and the journey? It was the beginning of the year, and January for that matter. Yet no salary. Opuliche had no pocket money. Travelling, packing and unpacking of things must be done. Moreover, feeding and washing all required some money.

The reverend sister had said that she would come at by 2 p.m. and if Opuliche was not ready then she would have to make her own arrangement to reach Onitsha. What else could this be if not mad haste? Inwardly, Opuliche was depressed, but the growing excitement of being called a college tutor did elevate her even there and then. And why not? Her fellow teachers had even started soliciting for her help in getting admission into the college at Emekuku. Somehow it was as if providence had directed its own people to be very kind to Opuliche in a very special way. So she did not remember any striking financial hardship in all those days. Even motor drivers proved very kind as if they were sent specially to help her.

Opuliche got to Onitsha and found some money to Betina home first and also return her cooking utensils since in the college teachers were provided food. The kind reverend mother had given her some money to pay the transport fare. Before leaving Onitsha, the supervisor of schools, Mother Catherine who gave Opuliche her fare, also gave her a letter of introduction to the principal of Emekuku Teachers Training College. This letter, she carefully put into one book to protect it from dirt and water.

Opuliche went to tell her mother's relations of these multiple transfers. One of her educated uncles, Fab, consoled her and encouraged her to get on with her work. However, when she told him about the letter a mad idea crept into their heads! Why not open it to make sure that the contents of the letter were not damaging? The letter was then bought out, made wet very carefully, and after due anxious moments and watchfulness, it was opened by the more careful of the two: Fab. The piece of paper read:

Convent Onitsha.
Jan. 1953

Dear Mother Bernard,
Here is Opuliche Okpato who should teach in your college. The report from Adazi College says that she is intelligent, capable and artistic, but needs supervision.

Yours,

Sis M Catherine

Opuliche and Fab were very worried about the 'but' in the letter. To them, it meant that Opuliche could not be trusted to carry out things on her own. In fact it was a slight on her character they surmised. Two heads are said to be better than one although we do not know if this is true at all times. The two heads had been very busy thinking out their solution for this *but* in the letter about Opuliche.

Opuliche thought of putting *although* in place of *but*. This idea was put off as *although* would make the sentence very loose. Then there was the thought of underlining the three positive words so they might outweigh the negative 'but needs supervision.' But they needed to find a similar ink. While on this search, they heard a loud knock sounded on the door and the letter was hurriedly put back into the book by an overwhelmed Opuliche whose heart was beating like that of a novice criminal.

Before ten o'clock that day, Opuliche was at Emekuku. It

was night, so the night-watch man was the person to welcome Opuliche to Emekuku. Before long, the students were carrying Opuliche's luggage into the dormitory, where she was to share their habitation. The idea of correcting the letter had long been abandoned when she rushed off from Fab's house with a guilty feeling. She felt guilty for tampering with the letter. Her heart was heavy because of her knowledge of what she interpreted to be an unfavourable report. With trembling in her heart she gave the letter immediately to the principal.

The principal was a very good woman by nature, and there and then, Opuliche felt that she should not have argued when she was asked to leave Dunukofia. Moreover she recalled that the day she had arrived Dunukofia, no student or even teacher's maids had come to help her with her loads. But here was she walking behind the students who were carrying all her belongings into the open hall. With a light curtain, Opuliche screened off her part of the large dormitory.

The staff of Emekuku Training College were mainly reverend sisters with only two other lay teachers Maggie and Vicky, and the new Opuliche. She made new friends at the college. There was Commy, a nurse, who used to bring Opuliche some food. The common food prepared for them in the college was not in the best taste always. This lady looked after Opuliche as a mother would. Opuliche also made a friend who had to live with her for three years. There was little Miss Beatrice, then in primary school at Emekuku Holy Rosary School. She lived with Opuliche as her maid.

In this college, there was just common meal, common bathroom, common toilet and room for both teachers and students. The difference was only that the three teachers were served the food first. This created room for the cooks to control the teachers. The tutors then being in the minority had to befriend the cooks so as to establish good rapport with them.

19

Emekuku

At Emekuku there was no opportunity for male and female intellectual interaction that Opuliche had wished for in life. Therefore she resorted to buying and reading novels. In addition, she was kept in the right course by the guidance of the principal. She was fond of staying with Opuliche and going out with her for legion work. Usually it was always two of them only, walking along the Emekuku road.

Opuliche could remember the very funny incident that happened just when she was about four days old in the college. She was quite alone in the teacher /kitchen room writing letters to friends. This room was used mainly for ironing clothes. She had made few friends from the many places she had lived in that year. She had signed the envelopes which were about seven in all. They were all spread on the large table in font of her. In the college at Adazi, where Opuliche had finished her training course, letters were strictly written only on

Sundays. These letters were passed to the reverend sister for supervision or to read before being sent out (as the student were meant to understand). This was to check if any letter were written to men or boys. Unconsciously then the students imbibed the idea that letter writing was bad. It was evil. Only bad girls wrote plenty letters. But having made some good friends, Opuliche was compelled to write them. At the same time, she did not want the principal to see her as a bad girl. So she sought out the lonely T/K room for her writing.

Since Opuliche arrived at the Emekuku to teach, she could not remember an hour which passed without her being in the company of this motherly principal. Surely before her seven letters were finished the principal would turn up. But Opuliche did not think of this probable fact as she was lost in the world of her letters. She was alone and felt quite secure in her solitude. Yet instinctively she dreaded Reverend Mother Mary Bernard coming. She had a thousand and one fearful thoughts that vehemently tormented her since she noticed that the reverend mother had taken a liking for her. Opuliche would not like this God-sent mother of hers to realise that she was so bad as, not just writing a letter, but writing so many at a time! And what was worse, writing these letters on a weekday and not on the permitted Sundays. These thoughts plagued her as she kept on writing.

At any rate, when she least expected it, the reverend mother was standing close to her. She took the addressed envelopes from the table as anybody who casually entered would be inclined to do. She looked at them one by one so very mechanically that she did not at all see the words written on them. Apparently the reverend sister was admiring the calligraphy. But Opuliche was dying of guilt and torment. She was worried with a multitude of destructive and terrifying imagination. She had always kept in mind the worst of that introductory letter about her. She would often repeat to herself *but needs supervision*! What else could all this closeness mean if not supervision. Yes, I need supervision, she condemned herself. For am I not here writing many letters, and on a day being Sunday?

Opuliche was about bursting out in a stream of apologies when the reverend mother probably sensing her unease left the room saying: 'I will come again.' But she never came back that afternoon. She had gone for her siesta. Opuliche seized the opportunity to find out from Miss Vicky whom to submit her letters for vetting before she could post them. She was surprised when Miss Vicky laughed at her and told her that such things were not observed here.

This was the mentality of the colonial mission teacher of the period with all the accompanying inhibition and inferiority complex. She was timid and full of mistrust like such other teachers of the period. The nerve had been stretched taut over the years in expectation of constant criticism. For the constant thing to expect was rebuke and reproof from superiors. Never a word of praise. The daily expectation of the victim was the inevitable reproach of evils that the next day must surely bring. The lower lip always protruded, helplessly bigger than the deserted upper one. The colonial mission teacher of the time had his belt or trouser band always loose and, from time to time, needed a deep inward adjustment. He had no hope anywhere as they told him of some reward somewhere in heaven. This used to give him solace at times. In his everyday life, the colonial mission teacher did live with a constant sense of guilt. He had been told not to read any other book except the book of his own section of the Christian denomination. It was mortal sin to research other materials. Opuliche's *She* a novel by Rider Haggard was confiscated by the mission school authorities. When Opuliche was taking tuition from the R.R.C London she was queried for receiving lecture materials not prescribed by church. At one time she was reading a psychology magazine booklet, and she was severely reprimanded for doing so. Of course, the authority promptly confiscated the booklets.

She could not go to Women Training College, Enugu which she had passed the qualifying examination because *our own* denominational college was deemed better. In any case, Opuliche could not go into any other college without the approval of her present school principal. Despite her excitement, she waited in vain for the signature of approval. The signature did not come. Opuliche had to get into *our own* college, whether there was any teacher there or not! This sense of guilt feeling did not stop with only reading books or reading in an institution that was not of *our own* faith. The colonial mission teacher had more shackles to confound her forever. She should not go to the house of or join her next door neighbour or brother to celebrate a marriage, birth or death. These were sinful! She must not marry somebody from or people of another faith, even from the same Christian belief. No. There was what was called denominations. Many female believers consequently remained unmarried. They were waiting for the right man from the same faith and he never appeared. Or worse, they got married to an unfeeling brute, a wicked animal walking with two legs and willing to marry the female in their church as was the case of Opuliche's friend Maria. From that wedding day, she knew Maria had entered hell while on earth. When maltreated and rough-handled as her husband did often, she would just take all as her 'penance.' She dared not look for change.

There was Romanus too. Romanus also found himself faced with such denominational marriage. Unfortunately for him, his wife had only a female child. Being African, he did not wish to put up with such a situation, yet he could not complain. His appearance grew progressively sad and his outlook very wicked as the years passed. While he contemplated his unspoken defeat in life, he would not talk of taking another wife because he still wanted people to regard him as good man. The mission teacher's worst ordeal was the division of brother so successfully done that if the civil war which drove away the missionaries had not happened, the little of what people called unity would have been impossible to achieve. The divide would have been greater culturally and otherwise she firmly believed.

Opuliche took her GCE ordinary level in Igbo when this division was acute. She passed quite all right but had to start learning the alphabet afresh when she found herself under a different set-up. Even the holy book, the Bible, had denominational disparities. Colonial mission teachers must not be free to read even the bible. He must first of all ask, 'am I free to read this?' The result would be that he would end up reading nothing for he had to wait for a reply that would never come. He must be overly careful and hesitant because all around him was full of: 'Don't, it is sinful!'

From hate and fear of supervision, Opuliche grew to hate all criticism. She took them all for overbearing supervision, watching, witch-hunting, disturbance or unwanted intrusion. She would be seen with the mouth pouting, just ready to oppose anybody that would as usual attempt to restrict or criticise her.

Opuliche proved excellent in art, drawing and painting. This was the artistic quality that was mentioned in the college report. Initially there were art lessons in Adazi College then given by one reverend sister Mary Perpetua, a tall, beautiful model. Opuliche did imitate this lady completely even in her gestures and mannerisms. Sister Mary Perpetua once commented on Opuliche's artistic sense which made Opuliche very happy.

She entered for art competition at the Adazi College. Many people took part: students, workers in the college, strangers, the former students of the institution, and many other people. After the competition Opuliche's drawing was judged best! She won a cash prize. As a result of this report on Opuliche a reverend sister Aggie came to Emekuku to seek her out. After consulting with the college principal, she told Opuliche that she wanted to open an apparatus centre for schools. Once again, Opuliche had to greet her friends 'bye bye.'

And so barely three months of coming to Emekuku, Opuliche experienced another change of station, this time from Emekuku to Nsu. Opuliche was to be the head of an institution: the art or apparatus centre.

When school re-opened in September that year, Opuliche was almost a whole principal in her own art school. Nsu was some twenty-one kilometres from Umuahia. Her little friend Beatrice, with her parent's consent, joined Opuliche at Nsu.

20

A Grease on Chains

Opuliche never overcame the negative impact of the words *but needs supervision* as she conceived them all through the times. Thus her emotions were always bottled up.

At Nsu, she had a whole block to herself. She was practically the principal of the centre, but under one reverend sister Mary Agnes. 'Here comes the supervision again,' she thought angrily. The tension was still high.

Unknown to her, freedom – total freedom – and personal responsibility was at the heart of Opuliche's inmost desires. The absence of this was nothing but chains around the feet and hands. Anyhow, there were some grease on the chains around Opuliche now for here she could at least eat what she liked. She could also live and sleep with her fellow teachers, instead of students as she had done at Emekuku and Adazi schools.

At Nsu, Opuliche experienced the joy and freedom of cooking for herself. She lived on her own at the teachers' quarters. At Agubaghara, she used to go to her apparatus centre block about one quarter of a mile from where she lived. She always went on a bicycle which she bought on August that very year. Not only this, she painted the bicycle with colours either to match or to contrast the original green of the bicycle.

Among her friends at the Nsu was Kate Akajiofor who became quite close to Opuliche. Kate was a higher elementary teacher. From Kate Akajiofor, Opuliche learnt several things about entertaining her visitors.

Nsu was a very good place indeed. She appreciated the melodious, whole hearted greetings of the people. It was like magic, for immediately Opuliche changed from cold social melancholy to warmth and robustness. In fact many Nsu men and women loved her. Many sought her advice on different areas of life. In time she had up to three godchildren.

She was in such a harmony with the people that to do any work in the apparatus centre compound was joy to them rather than a waste of their time. They all came as soon as Opuliche wanted them. Many non-Christians, especially old women and men, were among the intimate friends of Opuliche. The result was that some of this aged people started coming to church. In the evening, it was a joy for her to see very old women coming to say the holy Rosary with Opuliche.

For the first time she showed initiative in the many things that she did. She had been socially, mentally, emotionally and spiritually revitalised. She found it unbelievable that she could think and work by herself other than that imposed and regulated by the missionary authority. To her, although the authority was still there, it seemed so far away.

Again, this freedom and serenity was not to last long.

It happened that a Reverend Whitman, along with his boy Bianjo, was sent to be the parish priest of the area. It did not take long for friendship to develop between Bianjo and Meetum, Opuliche's house maid. One day, Meetum was cooking when Bianjo sent for her. The girl stayed too long in returning, and as a consequence, the soup burnt in the fire. Opuliche returned from the apparatus centre and was told what happened. Angrily she went to Bianjo and demanded for a sum of compensation for her burnt soup. This brought some misunderstanding and quarrel between the reverend's boy and Opuliche. At the height of the quarrel, she had the temerity to report the case to Reverend Whitman. Bianjo was offended that such a report had spoilt his good and 'holy' name. A whole Reverend Whitman's boy being connected with a sinful act. Reverend Whitman, from all indication felt as insulted as his boy. He felt twice annoyed that a black woman dared complain about his boy.

Reverend Whitman of course was the sole owner of the whole compound! At least so he said. The Reverend spoke. Opuliche was to pack out from the mission compound.

In indignation, she went to the reverend father to protest.

'What is it?' Reverend Whitman queried as soon as he saw her approaching with a small group of people.

'I want to know why I am being evicted,' Opuliche stammered, her strength suddenly deserting her.

'We can no longer condone your laxity in spiritual matters...'

'Laxity? What laxity?'

'For instance you were not at the morning mass this morning...'

'What!' Opuliche exclaimed, tears springing to her eyes. 'I was...'

'Are you calling me a liar?' the father asked menacingly. Everybody froze.

'No father, but I...,' she finished limply, looking at her companions for some kind of encouragement.

'Be sure to pack out of this compound before one o'clock,' the father snapped and entered his house in final dismissal.

Opuliche turned away with blinding tears. 'Oh, why do they always do this to me,' she burst out vehemently.

Whitman had succeeded in putting her on the defensive rather than discipline his boy. Thus her punishment for complaining about the reverend's boy was to lose her precious little house.

Later Bianjo was sent to teach typing at the apparatus centre. Opuliche was amazed at this arrangement because Bianjo had no qualification to teach the subject. But who was she to complain about such irregularities that abound in mission administration? She was more disturbed about the reverend father's intention in bringing Bianjo to be her staff. She gave him a typewriter as was the practice.

One day Bianjo's typewriter broke down and he went to carry Opuliche's own. She refused and a struggle ensued. Bianjo beat Opuliche with one of his crutches (Bianjo had only one leg, the other having been amputated). Opuliche broke the crutches into two. The man was mad. He hopped away amidst the jeer of the students whom he had terrorised with his crutches, having turned it into a handy cane to beat them with. The fight was not over as Opuliche was to find out soon. Quietly, Bianjo took time and planned his revenge.

One Friday afternoon, Opuliche was ill with malaria. She was so weak that she was made to lie in bed. The students were all out in the field cutting grass and playing. Bianjo saw his opportunity. He calmly slipped into the room as if to tell her 'sorry.' When he saw how helpless Opuliche looked, he quietly locked the door and brought out some rubber wires. Before Opuliche could move from her reclining position, the brute attacked. Opuliche screamed and yelled in pain. She was defenceless against the onslaught of lashes that descended upon her.

A few students who heard her muffled cries came running. Magdalene Anamekwa, one of Opuliche's strong students jumped into the room through the window and grappled with Bianjo. Others came and helped her in restraining Bianjo's hands. When Bianjo saw that he was overpowered, he fled the room, leaving his bag and books behind.

The case was promptly reported to the white reverend sister 'supervising' the apparatus centre. Surprisingly, she did nothing. Rather one day, while the teachers were all in class she visited. She went to inspect Opuliche's quarters. Later that day when Opuliche returned, she discovered that Bianjo's bag and books, which she had kept as evidence, had vanished from her room.

Opuliche often wondered at these white so-called

119

missionaries who seemed to take delight in the quarrels of their employees. Many questions formed in her mind. Why did they not want to make peace for the people working under them? Were all these religious people really good people? On the other hand, did they often provide shackles that will chain and inhibit people under them? Were they really workers for God whom Opuliche and others of the time believed they were?

At Nsu, Opuliche continued her self tuition and private preparation for the GCE qualifying test. She contented herself with her numerous friends and well-wishers. Why then should the hostility of Bianjo, or little Meetum's lewdness, or even the cold arrogance of white people, bother her so much? Also near Opuliche at Nsu was Opuliche's relation Charles Okpato. Charles was managing a small catering house at Orieagu. Opuliche had helped him to set up this business. The people so trusted her sense of judgement that she would even decide marriage disputes!

Really, Opuliche had great influence at that time. She was in charge of so many things.

But all that was soon to change.

It happened that Opuliche had to take some students to Obowo for artwork. She requested for money from the reverend sister in charge for feeding the students. She was told that the money would be given her at Obowo. At Obowo, the reverend sister did not provide the money for feeding the students.

'What do we do then?' Opuliche asked in exasperation.

'Oh, find a way and manage,' replied the sister entering her

Volkswagen Beetle car.

'But, I've told you I do not have any money,' Opuliche was quite close to tears.

There was no response from the sister.

'Move,' she commanded her driver instead. But the car would not move. Opuliche had held on to the door of the car with all her strength. She held fast to the vehicle with such anger that the vehicle could not move. People gathered to watch the drama. The woman ordered the driver to stop as Opuliche was now in tears,

'I said we do not have any money. What do we do?' she asked the sister. The angry sister again told her driver to move. And they drove off.

However Opuliche's action attracted the attention of some sympathisers who contributed money for her wards' feeding.

Two weeks after this incident, a punitive letter of transfer was sent to Opuliche. This transfer was a calculated inconvenience as the year was then almost at an end. It was meant just to sow the seed of insecurity in the mind of the hopeless mission teacher, especially the one working under the reverend sisters of the period. The main idea was to keep the colonial mission teacher always insecure, anxious and afraid. The Nigerian government public service also copied this tactics from their white mentors. The keynote then was on the restriction, intimidation, threat and snobbery of the humble mission teachers. All their expression should be that of unhappiness, timidity and want. The good works were rewarded in heaven. Only bad teachers demanded their right.

That was why the punishment came. Opuliche had demanded money for feeding the students who were out of station.

Opuliche went on transfer to Ihite Holy Rosary School. There, all the teachers were happily living in one open hall. She, unlike them, had owned chairs, bed, and other household furniture. While all the other female teachers were contented to live in one large open hall (at least nobody complained), Opuliche expressed her reservation about this type of accommodation.

Early in the month of December, the school year ended. While Opuliche was busy carrying all her property, the others simply took their boxes, pails, and few items for their toiletries, then off they dashed! Christmas vacation! It was a day's labour for Opuliche. The mission school management had decided to house all the teachers together in a common big room. This would make for very cheap and easy management. Yes, management of underlings which the mission teachers of the colonial times had become. This arrangement also made impossible for the teachers to think of accumulating any personal property of their own. Thus they were content with the stipends they were paid.

21

Uboma School Adventure

Opuliche had very earlier been told that her mother's last request before dying was that nothing should distract her attention from her studies. Her father had joined in this wish. Opuliche therefore cultivated the company of intellectual friends like Ugu and Ije. These people motivated her to read. Although Ije was simply a teacher when they met, his love for education made him persevere in his studies and within a short time, he became a professor. Opuliche was particularly impressed by this academic achievement. These people became her advisers. Therefore, she put in for the General Certificate of Education examination and a tuition course from Rapid Results College, London.

Her love for education made her highly selective in her choice of friends. It was not surprising therefore that she was mostly alone. After a while as classroom teacher, Opuliche went away to train as higher elementary school teacher.

She went to Uboma College to complete her teaching course. There she met Ogbonna, who was a staff of the college. Ogbonna had gone overseas for her studies. Opuliche was impressed that a woman could achieve this feat at such a time. Opuliche also took tuition from the Pitman's Correspondence College, for fine arts. Before this time, she had been buying and reading books, mostly novels, to keep herself busy. She used to record the books she had read in a diary. In her entries, she would write the name of the book, when she started reading and when she finished. In addition, she would copy out good expressions she found in such books. This way, she aimed at self-improvement. She registered for the qualifying test for English language and passed. This gave her greater confidence in herself and her abilities.

A year later, Opuliche took five subjects in the G.C.E. Examination at Onitsha. She entered for seven subjects but was only able to take five. Having had no real teachers in Geography and Mathematics, she discovered that she could not write the examinations on these subjects. It was only in the primary school that she was taught these subjects. The training colleges she attended felt that girls had no use for these subjects since they had no direct bearing on marriage and home management. It was highly ambitious for Opuliche to enter for subjects like Mathematics, Geography, History, English Language, Fine Arts Igbo and Religious knowledge in that very 1955 June G. C. E. Examination. She was on such a shaky educational background yet Opuliche took only six months to establish a pattern for her studies. Her mates nicknamed her Martin Luther. Studying Geography and Mathematics without any aid proved very trying for her. She quietly dropped these subjects.

After the June 1955 G. C. E. Examination, Opuliche was quite elated. She felt she had scored a milestone in her academic pursuit. It did not matter to her whether she passed or not, but her participation in the examination was most important to her. In fact the school manager, Reverend Sister Mary Michel was so impressed by Opuliche's consistent and undaunted academic efforts that she planned an overseas educational course for Opuliche.

Opuliche was told that she would go to Buckingham Palace, London, to do a course with a bias in fine arts. Opuliche was excited.

Some few months later, Opuliche's prospects suffered a blow. One day, John, the manager's driver, called Opuliche into the reverend sister's house and relayed the bad news. The reverend manager Michel was with reverend sister Mary Roseri who was Opuliche's 1948 Adazi school Manager. The subject of their discussion was Opuliche. Both of them told the story why Opuliche's overseas course was no longer feasible. In a nutshell, the story was that one Miss Ogle, an education officer, who should authenticate Opuliche's application, said that if Opuliche had been a *higher* elementary teacher instead of just the elementary teacher, all would have been okay. Opuliche being only an ETC, Miss Ogle, would not want to apply for something that she very well knew that nobody could support. The reverend sisters told Opuliche that the telegram on this matter was received the previous night. They suggested to Opuliche to get ready to enter a new college to be opened by the manager soon.

But one day when the reverend manager was particularly irritated by Opuliche's iconoclastic profile, she burst out that it was because of her stubbornness that they had cancelled her overseas training programme.

'You would have gone there and changed the course which we sent you to study!'

When Opuliche left her office, she went to ask people the meaning of changing course. She was told that the sisters were afraid that once she found herself in a London institution she would change from the small home economics subject to a more lucrative course like law or medicine. Opuliche smiled sadly. So it was not Miss Ogle or any higher elementary requirement. She became very thoughtful. No wonder the suggestion that day that she must go to a new college to do a completion course. The college was for higher elementary training for girls. Perhaps they were afraid of the subjects that she entered for in GCE. The whole disappointment made her resolve to get higher elementary qualification.

Opuliche had been disappointed when she was told that her overseas academic programme could not take place. However, she was bitter when she learnt that these sisters schemed the whole thing. On August of that year, Opuliche ran into Nnadozia, her PTA chairman at Nsu. He was by then an education assistant. He was congratulating Opuliche on her prospective overseas course when he learnt of the disappointment and her resolve to get the required higher elementary certificate. Nnadozia offered to go that day to fill the form for Opuliche so that she could take the H.E. examination that was fast approaching. It was a hurried business of the most dextrous nature. But she succeeded in sitting for that examination with other candidates.

The results came out. Immediately after lessons, the students took permission to go to Umuahia Education office to look at the list. Most of them passed single subjects. Opuliche passed all the subjects. Others failed both subjects. Anyhow this did not matter much. The full-passed Opuliche, the half-passed and the failed people were all to complete their two-year course at Uboma. Opuliche, in the privacy of her room, rejoiced and thanked God. It was quite a spectacular moment in her life. She was very happy.

Life at Uboma for Opuliche was quite steady. There were no financial setbacks this time for Opuliche and her classmates were being paid their full salary. Above all, there was no death in Opuliche's family. Instead, more children were born into the family by her stepmother. This was unlike her first college experience.

In this college, students may write letters and nobody read their letters. Thus Opuliche was able to plan overseas tuition in English Literature and English History at advanced G.C E. This was why the principal at one stage started to call Opuliche Miss GCE. The popular name her fellow students had for Opuliche, however, was Contra (rebel).

Uboma College did not have steady teachers. Some teachers stayed only for a month and left. There were some that came on vacation jobs there. Among these was Hyacinth Ugwu. To Opuliche, he was the best teacher of whole lot. It was by Ugwu's encouragement that Opuliche began to like Geography. Uboma College was the first college that Opuliche and many others in her class had the right idea of this subject called Geography. He actually awakened in her the desire to read any book on Geography with real interest. All the class appeared to realise the good work Ugwu was doing for them regarding this Geography. When he was to leave them at the end of the three months vacation job, the whole class mourned his departure. They bought a book for him to mark their appreciation of his efficient work.

Before Ugwu, the students only had a young woman teaching this subject. This woman tried to struggle over the Geography period by placing both her two hands, palms spread out on top of the map by way of showing the class the position of a particular country. What a way to teach! With her hand covering a large portion of the map, she would then announce to the class; 'This is London.' But Mr Ugwu's arrival had brought out the yawning inefficiency of this teacher. Poor thing! Although she tried her best, she only succeeded in confusing the students. But she was not alone.

In Arithmetic, the teacher would write on the board: 2+1=3 2+2=4 2+3=5. She was teaching Arithmetic just as she taught English.

Many teachers taught their subjects in such less than fortunate manner. It was only in History and Principles of Education, the two subjects which Ogbonna persistently taught the class, that students in the college developed some confidence in. Before long, Ogbonna had to go away thus worsening the unstable academic level of Uboma College. That was the new college that the reverend sisters had recommended for Opuliche, instead of Buckingham Palace.

How about the results at the end of the course?

All the class, except one student, failed. Yet all the students in that class did well in Principles of Education which Ogbonna taught!

Before Ogbonna left, Opuliche had struck a chord of friendship with her. For five days, Opuliche stayed with this woman. She was greatly influenced by this good teacher. She was one of the best Christians and educated women that Opuliche had ever seen. Ogbonna's influence on Opuliche was not only on the academic field. Opuliche also visited her home and was impressed by the orderly way things moved in the household. Opuliche saw how Ogbonna looked after her aged parents and other brothers and sisters as if she were the man of the house in the African manner of speaking.

When the Uboma result of December 1957 came out Opuliche was the only successful person. Miss Ogbonna said that she was not surprised. This spectacular result from the teacher training Uboma, did much for Opuliche. It encouraged her to read harder. Not only that Opuliche was the only person who passed, she passed at Credit level. This result gave her a lot of confidence. She took a photograph with the certificate to commemorate the event. In fact, the next result from the college, which was the one of December 1958, recorded a complete zero pass! Nobody at all passed from that institution. How could they, when the students were not properly taught. No wonder government education authorities after the civil war relegated the institution from a teacher training to just a secondary school.

Love of learning made Opuliche buy herself a giant reading lamp in December. While she bought other gift items for her relations, she bought herself a lamp for reading in the night. With the lamp, she was out of bed as early as 4 a.m. each morning in her small room attached to the main building of her late father's house. She read with a purpose. In June/July the next year she would be taking London G. C. E. Advanced level. She was confident and full of superior airs. She had no time for idle talks. She kept a simple appearance and shunned all types of embellishments on hair, body or clothing. Those were a waste of time and money.

Still reading without any formal coaching, she nearly passed the two papers that year. She had 37 and 39 marks for English Literature and History respectively, while 40 was just the pass mark limit of the G.C.E. Advanced Level Examination that time. Rather than become depressed, she was further encouraged by the result to study harder. As a result of her performance, she was awarded Ordinary level passes in the two subjects. She reapplied for the same examination the next year. This time, she added Latin to make her subject three. She was teaching under the Catholic Mission the Holy Rosary Sisters.

As was the practice, she was being transferred almost every month. This did not help her academic ambition at all. Still she persevered.

Opuliche took and passed the qualifying test to enter the university in 1960. After her associate diploma in education course at Ibadan in 1961, Opuliche continued her self-tuition. She still wanted to get the advanced level pass in the subjects that she had chosen: English Literature and History. This time she put Religious Knowledge in place of Latin, to make her subjects still three the requisite to do a degree course in the university.

In January 1965, Opuliche's dream came true. She actually passed in three subjects in the London G.C.E. at Advanced Level. By this time, Opuliche was at Enugu, teaching as a civil servant teacher. She had access to a library and even educational pictures and movies that helped her in her studies. Not only that, she had got a steady station in the civil service, no more routine transfers every month. She could read without fear! Yes, fear that the manager might not like her if she read and may call her either Martin Luther or Miss GCE, and also ostracise her in indirect ways. Other teachers were so carefully guided from her influence that she had begun to wonder if she was not doing a bad thing by wanting to read. That was Opuliche's experience: dilemma in the dark, with nobody to talk with.

But now as government employee, all those inhibitions were

gone. As a civil servant teacher, Opuliche was surprised to notice that she was paid to travel and take examinations. Opuliche was told this and at once she stopped hiding the tuition papers from people at the government school, a practice beginning from her encounter with the missionary sisters. At Enugu she learnt with relief that teachers were encouraged to read and take examinations, as this learning will reflect on the performance rating of the teacher. Opuliche was told that women did not usually pass English Literature at Advanced Level. Instead of being discouraged, this very statement made her put in more energy in her preparation for the examination.

22

Proud Undergraduate

In 1965 the result came out and she passed all the three papers she registered. She got the three papers at Advanced Level in one sitting. Such a rare feat! She was really happy and proud of herself. Before this time, she had been denied admissions into the three universities in the country. However, with this outstanding academic performance, all the three universities admitted her into their degree programmes. University of Nigeria, Nsukka offered her Psychology. University of Lagos gave her admission to read English. University of Ibadan offered her admission to do a degree programme in History. Opuliche was highly elated. A beggar did have a choice at last. She was no longer begging for admission; she had three universities to pick her choice. In her legitimate pride, she chose Ibadan, her former university.

While at the Enugu British Council library, Opuliche had read and swallowed, as it were, a book called; *The Seven Ages of*

Woman by Elizabeth Parker. This book taught her a lot of things about the life of women. Thus she held the view that life should be broadened, balanced and diversified. She felt it was time she gave attention to her body. This book, among others, helped liberate her views on the relationship between the sexes. Clothes with brighter colours began to fill the boxes of the former drab *acada* girl. Even trinkets and cosmetics were this time admired at the shops. Yet Opuliche never could forget reading. She had a daily reading timetable that she mounted on a chart.

When the time arrived, Opuliche travelled to Ibadan University for her second time studies in September that 1965. Where many students had to change lorries and cars, Opuliche had a 404 car from Enugu to Ibadan all by herself. This was made possible because of the support of her godfather, Nwankwo. It was a big contrast to her first departure to Ibadan University five years ago. This time, Opuliche was in her life's economic boom. Things were easy and comfortable for her because of the civil servant job and her Enugu environment.

Life at Ibadan this time was really very different from that of the 1960/61 diploma course period. In 1965 there was rest of mind and relaxation. Opuliche had plenty of property like sewing machine, electric fan and other household items as opposed to the 1960/61 experience when she went with nothing but a haggard life of want. Then Opuliche could not afford, but made, her own clothes hanger. She made them with a stick and a rope. But this time she was relaxed. She could even find the antics of the cartoonist in the *Bug and Scorpion* very funny. Along with other qualified students, Opuliche matriculated in November 6 that 1965. She was at last doing a degree course. But that was not what mattered to her, she still had English, History, and French as her first year subjects.

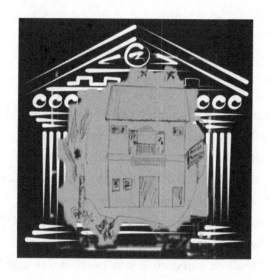

Named after Modiba

The extra care Opuliche took of her body did not go unnoticed. Naturally gifted with a pretty looking figure, it was not long, after she had made up her mind to settle down, that she finally said *yes* to the man of her choice. He definitely did not hail from her home town, Ogu, who swore that book was her husband. In justifying her choice to *her* relatives Opuliche remarked he was the type that encouraged her to read.

When Opuliche's first child was born, it was a male child. Mama Angelina, Opuliche's old aunt, consulted the native doctor as they used to do and it was said that Opuliche's son was the spirit of Opuliche's father Dobendu. When the second issue of Opuliche came and was a female, Opuliche was confident that at last she had a way of remembering her mother, Modiba. She believed that, as her son was her father, this daughter must of course be her mother.

There was the usual consultation of the local oracle by Opuliche's aunt. Contrary to Opuliche's expectations, the new female child was not Opuliche's mother! Mama Angelina said that according to the oracle, the female child was the spirit of her own mother. Even though Angelina was the sister of Opuliche's father, Opuliche was not happy that her own mother Modiba was being side-tracked in the scheme of things.

From that day, Opuliche started to think that this woman who used to get the 'truth' from the oracle, must have not been a good friend of Mohiba. 'Otherwise, why should the oracle say that the son was my father while this next one was not my mother?

'Perhaps the problem was with the oracle.'

So in baptising the child, Opuliche called her Modiba. The name Modiba, added to the child's own name, was to honour Opuliche's mother. To her, the little baby girl was Modiba and no other. The woman she had known and loved for some time in her life had every reason to return to her.

To immortalise Modiba still, Opuliche finished building her house at Aba and she put up a billboard on which was boldly written: *MODIBA MEMORIAL MONTAGE.*